Journeys

J L Coates

Other Books by the Author

Judith Coates – Be Who You Be

     Let Your Light Shine

     my life, my story with Beyond the

         Heart Clubhouse

J L Coates – Second Chances

     Awakening

     Two Women, Two Stories

     Shattered

     The Seeker, the Sentinel and the Orb

     Total Equals the Sum of the Parts

     A Change of Heart

     Journeys

Library and Archives Canada in Publication

 J L Coates

ISBN:978-1-7751668-0-1

Printed in USA by KDP

Cover photo by Judy Coates

DEDICATION

To the pioneer women who formed the foundation of our great country - including Lydia Ratke, Rachel Naughton, Pearl Wald and Julia Coates, four truly amazing women who accomplished so much with so little. You are my heroes!

ACKNOWLEDGMENTS

The people, names and places used in this story are fictional. Any likeness to those living is purely coincidental. Some of the incidents are loosely based upon the truth, others on hearsay. Either way, this story is a product of my overactive imagination.

My grandparents, who were German and lived in a small town in Saskatchewan, were discriminated against, as were their children. The scars of which never did heal. My dad did have a brother who went to work on the Alaska Highway. That was the last his family knew of him, and to the day they died my dad and my uncle longed to find him.

A good story revolves round the question "what if". In this the story the question is "what if two women, years apart in age, find an answer to the same question what happened to Ivan?"

In 2005 Alberta Centennial funds were made available to communities to record their local history. I used several of these books as background information on the time and culture. Thank you to the many men and women who devoted their time to sharing the past and making it available for the future.

If we look back times have not changed. These immigrants came to Canada seeking a better life for themselves and their children and settled our country. I thank them for their determination and bravery. Without them, few of us would be where we are today.

Thanks to Clarice Nelson for being my beta reader. Your suggestions are always right on.

I also wish to thank Dianne Tchir for editing this manuscript, and for her faith and belief in me. Without her encouragement I would have given up a long time ago.

CONTENTS

Fortitude is the strength of mind

that allows one to endure pain

and adversity with courage.

* * *

Memory, like Ivy, clings to olden times

and things and ways.

Land of Hope and Dreams
Page 745

One

Clutching the support railing on the wall with one hand the old lady shuffled down the hallway to the glass Solarium of the nursing home. Early every morning she made the same journey, carrying a black bag with a Think Green logo on the side. From here she could look out upon the ripening field of wheat and the stands of green trees in the distance. Through the glass she thought she could feel the warmth of the sun on her face and the gentle breeze on her skin.

Settling into her favourite chair, the green paisley one with the high back and two solid arms, she leaned back and closed her eyes. She always chose this chair because her feet touched the floor, and it was easy to get out of. Today, the short trip down the hall had left her panting and feeling short of breath. *I am tired today. Elyse and I had such a big day yesterday and it was fun. I don't know if she knows how much I appreciated going back to our old place.*

After several minutes she opened her eyes. Reaching down into her bag she pulled out her black coiled scribbler and pen, and began writing laboriously. *This takes much longer since I had my stroke. My hand has a hard time grasping the pen. Everything I do seems to takes twice as long to do than it used to.*

. After her stroke almost all of her movement had come back, but she was still having some trouble talking. The words were there, on the tip of her tongue, but she had to think for a long time to get them out. This frustrated her as well as her family.

Her hand no longer moved as freely as it used to, but she still able to write in her journal every day. She thought about her Aunt Perpetua, who had made, then given her the first journal when she was ten. On the first page her aunt had written, "Write down your thoughts. They are the one thing you truly own."

In her room, at the foot end of her bed was her great-grandfather's carved wooden chest which held all of the journals that she had saved throughout the years. *Somebody might want them when I am gone.*

"How is it going today Mrs. Walker?" The nice nurse Sally Moro asked as she came into the solarium with a cup of tea and her morning pills. She liked Sally and was pleased she was engaged to her grandson Carl. They made a nice couple.

"Looks like it is going to be another beautiful day," Sally added. "Perhaps later I will come to get you and you can sit outside on the patio and enjoy the sunshine. I know how much you love that. Does that sound like a good idea?"

She took the pills Sally offered, and watched as she opened a folding table, and placed her tea upon it.

"Yes, I would like that," she replied.

Putting her book and pen back into her bag she once again leaned her head back and closed her eyes. Drifting off, she thought about how, when she lived on the farm, she had spent most of her time outdoors. Now she had to wait for someone to wheel her into the sunshine.

Sally found her half an hour later sitting in her chair, head back, and a smile on her face.

Sarah was unaware of Sally's call for help, the ambulance ride to the hospital, or the frantic arrival of her children. She was travelling back to another place and to another time.

Two

Elyse Walker yawned as she saw the sign post – CLARION- 5 miles. She was tired after driving for thirty-six hours and covering three thousand miles. Even though she stayed at a hotel the night before and had a fairly decent sleep, she felt as though she couldn't drive another mile. Besides, this was the first time she travelled by herself with only a roadmap as a guide.

The closer she was to her destination the higher her anxiety level. Would she find what and who she was looking for? Was she wasting her time, money, and energy on a wild goose chase? The faded picture she had found was at least fifty years old, if not more.

She turned right, and within minutes the town of Clarion was ahead of her. The sign read population thirty-five hundred, and showed what amenities were available. Underneath some graffiti artist had written "counting dogs and cats."

The most prominent feature was a water tower, reaching high into the sky line. Up ahead she saw another sign that said Reindeer Lodge. She turned into the parking lot to see if there were any rooms available.

All her life her grandfather had told stories about his parents and his life on the farm, but each time he was asked why they didn't come to see or contact him, he would refuse to answer. He was like that, always changing the subject when he didn't want to talk about something.

His dying words still echoed in her head, "I thought she would come. Keep trying Elyse, I need to tell her I am sorry."

Up until his last breath he kept asking, "Is she here yet?" This hope of his mother coming made her feel that her grandfather had suffered longer than he needed to.

Every time she thought about him she became angry. Yet, when she put her anger aside, there was a spot inside her that felt incomplete- like some part of her was missing. Even as a child she sensed her grandfather's sadness when he spoke of his childhood. There were so many unanswered questions.

She had found the picture in his drawer while helping her mother pack up her Grandfather's house. Because the writing on the back was so faded she could barely make out the names on the back – Sarah, Henry and Clarion. Holding the picture in her hand she went into the kitchen where her mom was packing dishes.

"Have you ever seen this picture before?" Elyse asked,

handing it to her mother. "Í wonder who these people are."

Her mother looked at the picture, and then turned it over "I have no idea, I haven't seen this one before, but I remember your grandfather telling us something about a town with that name once. I think it was close to where he grew up – some place in Canada."

"Do you think these could be his parents?"

"I have no idea Elyse. I never knew their names."

"Mom, can I keep this picture?"

"I don't see why not. As it is I don't know what we are going to do with all this stuff. Once everyone has taken what they want I am going to suggest to your dad that we put the rest into an auction sale."

From there it was easy. A brief search on her computer, and she discovered several towns named Clarion, but only one was in the northern Canada, and had the name Henry Walker in the Internet phone directory.

She knew it wasn't much to go on, but here she was. If they were dead, at least she would have seen a lot of beautiful country. She thought about calling the phone number she found but if it was disconnected she would be no further ahead. *The only way to find out for sure is to go there.*

Several weeks after her grandfather's passing her mother handed her a cheque for Twenty-five thousand dollars.

"What are you going to do with your money Elyse" she asked.

"You probably won't like to hear what I have in mind."

"Which is what?"

"I can't stand the thought that nobody from Grandfather's family was here with him when he died. I am having a hard time understanding how people can be that way. I want to take some of the money and go find them."

"Why would you want to do that? What will it prove? Whatever happened so long ago is better left alone."

"Mom, he laid there begging for his mother, waiting for her to come and there was nothing we could do. Until I found that picture we had no idea where they could be. I know it doesn't give me much information but I feel like I have to do this for him."

Her mother looked at her, "what is the rest of your reason? I have a feeling you are holding something back."

"What do you mean?" Elyse asked.

"I know you well enough to know you are thinking of more than that. Your face always gives you away."

"Grandpa had a heart of gold and would have given you the shirt off his back if you asked for it. I feel like I need to know who his family was, what happened, and why they weren't there for him. There is part of me that feels empty-like something is missing. I don't know how else to explain it."

Her mother was quiet for several seconds. "I am not surprised you feel this way. It's your money; you can spend it however you want. You know, it could end up being a wild goose chase."

"I know mom, but I feel like I have to try. Grandfather was a good man, a little crude at times and rough around the edges, but he didn't deserve to be ignored."

"Did you ever stop to think that maybe that was his choice Elyse?"

"Maybe it was, but I need to find out for myself."

Elyse was on summer break from college where she was studying journalism. She talked to the editor of the local paper about documenting her trip and he had agreed to pay her for each article she sent in.

So here she was in Clarion determined to find her grandfather's family and tell them what she thought of them. Her grandfather had been the best a girl could ask for. No matter what family differences there may have been, none of it should have mattered when he was dying.

First she had to a place to stay and get something to

eat. After that she would come up with a plan. Right now all she wanted was a bed. Tomorrow would be soon enough to start searching for her great-grandparents. *It will be a miracle if they are still alive but I may be able to find other family members.*

The first thing she did the next morning was dial the phone number she had found on the internet. "Sorry this number is no longer in service," the voice said

"Crap," Elise said out loud, "that would have been too easy."

She opened the top desk drawer and found a phone book. There were all kinds of Walker names, but none with the initial H. After breakfast she drove to the main street, and parked her car in front of the bank. Right beside the bank was the town office. Opening the front door she went inside. *This seems as good a place as any to start.*

"May I help you," the receptionist asked.

"Yes, I am new in town, and I am looking for Henry and Sarah Walker."

"Sorry, I am fairly new here myself and don't recognize the name."

"Thanks anyway," Elise replied. "Guess I have to keep on trying."

The next two businesses she tried the result was the

same. Finally she went into the drugstore and spoke to the clerk there. "I am trying to find my great-grandparents Henry and Sarah Walker. Do you happen to know them?"

"Yes, I know who they are. Henry died a few years ago, and I'm not sure what happened to Sarah. My dad's in the back, maybe he will know. Follow me." She led Elyse to an older, white haired man standing behind the pharmacist counter.

"Hey dad, you got a minute. This lady is looking for Henry and Sarah Walker? I know Henry died, but do you know what happened to Sarah? Is she dead too?"

The man looked at her and asked, "why are you looking for them?'

"I want to see if they are my great-grandparents. My grandfather's name was Ivan Walker. He died just over a month ago, and I'm looking for his family so I can tell them. *That*; *and give them a piece of my mind.*

"There are lots of Walker boys, but I don't ever recall of hearing of one called Ivan. Henry, he died about five years ago. Sarah, she sold the house and moved into the Green Gable Lodge. Don't know for sure she is still there or not. You can try there I guess."

"Did you know them at all?"

"Not really, just the name. I have only been here for about seven years myself."

"Where do I find the Green Gables Lodge?"

"If you came in from the south you would've passed it on your right."

"Thank you." Elyse said.

She walked back to the car, her stomach tied up in knots. *If I find Sarah, what is she going to say or what is she going to do? I guess the worst that can happen is she tells me to leave.*

She drove back to the highway she had driven into town, and spotted the complex right away. There was an archway supported by rock pillars, and across the arch a sign that read Green Gable Lodge. Entering the property she noticed a sign that said 'you are here.'

She got out of the car walked over to the sign which turned out to be a road map of the complex. She studied it for several minutes and returned to her car.

Turning left, as the sign indicated she noticed the buildings were in units of four with flowers on either side of the concrete sidewalk. Each Unit had white shutters and was painted a bright color. Large mature trees lined the street, and the manicured lawns led from one to the other.

Further ahead she noticed a building with a bright blue ramp and a large deck on one side. Picnic tables sat under large shady trees. At one two men sat obviously playing a game of some sort.

The parking lot was half empty so there was no problem finding a spot close to the front door.

Getting out of the car she wiped her hands down the side of her legs and took a deep breath. She walked through the front door and followed a sign which pointed to the reception area. *I think I am going to be sick. What if I have come all this way for nothing?*

Taking a deep breath she began walking toward the desk. Suddenly a voice asked "can I help you?"

Startled Elyse turned around, "I am looking for Sarah Walker. I was told she might live here."

"Why yes, she is in room two twelve – down the hallway to your right. Do you want me to show you?"

"No I'm sure I can find it myself. Thank you."

As Elyse made her way down the long hallway she saw a library with a fireplace and comfortable chairs on one side. Next to it was a common dining area. On the other side was a large games room where she could hear men laughing, and beside it a small chapel. The colors were bright and cheery and everything looked spotlessly clean.

In front of room two twelve she took another deep breath and knocked on the door.

"Come in," an older woman's voice called out.

Elyse opened the door and took one step into the

room. An elderly white-haired woman walked toward her. Elyse immediately recognized her as an older version of the woman in the picture in her purse.

"May I help you Dearie? Are you lost?"

"No," Elyse answered, "I have come a long way looking for somebody. By any chance are you Sarah Walker?"

"Yes, that's my name."

"Did you have a son named Ivan?"

"Yes, but he has been dead for more than sixty years already, why do you ask?"

"Mrs. Walker, my name is Elyse Walker; my grandfather's name was Ivan Henry Walker."

The lady staggered, reaching for the edge of the door to keep from falling. Her face turned white, and she was visibly shaking, "You must have the wrong person. My Ivan is dead; we lost him during the war."

Elise crossed the distance between them in a few steps. Taking Sarah's arm, she led her to the closest chair. "Are you okay Mrs. Walker? Should I call someone?"

"I am fine – just give me a minute to catch my breath."

Sarah studied the girl standing in front of her. She was tall with black spiky hair, an earring in her eyebrow, and what looked like a diamond in her left nostril. She had deep blue eyes like Ivan's and Henry's.

"You said your name was Elyse, what makes you think Ivan might be my son?"

"This picture," Elyse replied.

Taking the old black-and-white picture from her purse she handed it to Sarah, and then she turned it over and said "there are four words on the back – Henry, Sarah Walker and Clarion." Her heart was hammering in her chest.

"Mrs. Walker, is this you?" Elyse asked, pointing to the woman in the picture.

Three

"Mrs. Walker, you are going to feel a sharp little prick in your arm. I am going to take some blood to run some tests. Try not to move for me."

There was tightness around my arm, a little pinch, and then the voice said "good girl. We are all done here."

"Gram, I am here too" said a younger voice that I couldn't quite recognize. "I am going to stay with you for a while until Rachel comes back."

Oh it's Elyse, she didn't have to come here and sit with an old lady, how nice of her.

Then the sounds disappeared and she was thinking about her oldest son Ivan. *More than sixty years have passed since I last saw him. Then, one day, this strange young girl knocks on the door of my room announcing she was Ivan's granddaughter. I knew it as soon as I saw her. I think it was her eyes.*

"Are you Sarah Walker?" she asked me.

I nodded yes.

"Did you have a son named Ivan?"

I nodded yes again.

"My name is Elyse Walker. Ivan was my grandfather."

I looked at her vaguely for a long time. She was tall and slim with a black spiky hair cut. She had an earring in her eyebrow and something shiny in her nose. My heart was pounding, a mist settled in front of my eyes. Was it really possible that my son Ivan had not died during the war?

"My Ivan is dead. We lost him during the war. You must have the wrong person."

She came in the door and crossed over to me. She must have seen the look of shock on my face and noticed I was trembling like a leaf.

"Are you okay Mrs. Walker? Should I call someone?"

I shook my head no and stared into her face. Yes, I could see the resemblance more clearly. She had the same deep blue eyes that Henry and Ivan both had.

I held out my arms and she folded into them, both of us cried. I knew all along, in my heart, that Ivan was alive. A mother knows these things.

Finally she pulled away and said, "I brought a picture to show you." Digging into her purse she pulled out a faded picture. "Is this you and your husband Henry?"

I remember the day Ivan took that picture. He saved his money for a long time and used it to buy a Brownie box camera. There was Henry dressed in bib overalls over a plaid shirt. He was handsome, but why is he looking so stern?

Look at me! I don't remember him being that much taller than me; I barely come up to his shoulders. I must have been working in the garden that day, because I have no shoes on. I loved the feel of the warm dirt on my bare feet. I remember that old faded house dress too. At the time I only had two dresses to my name, this one and my Sunday church dress.

Look, there is the back door of our old log house. I kept the rain barrel there to get water for my flowers.

Yes. This is us. I remember that day so clearly. Would you please go tell the nurse to phone my daughter Rachel to come here? I want her to see this.

When she came back Clara Armstrong, the head nurse, was with her.

"How are you doing Mrs. Walker? This young lady tells me you have had a bit of a shock."

I nodded yes. Clara fussed around for a while, taking my pulse and blood pressure.

"Everything is fine. I called Rachel like you wanted and she should be here any minute."

She had no sooner got those words out of her mouth when Rachel walked in, as huffy as usual.

"What is going on here?" Then turning to Elyse, she asked, "Who are you?"

"This is Ivan's granddaughter Elyse."

"Not that again mom, Ivan is dead, you know that."

"No. She has a picture of your dad and me that Ivan took."

"Mom, for heaven's sake, she could be anybody and got that picture from who knows where." then, looking at Elyse she said coldly, "you can leave any time."

"No" I said again, "Elyse do you mind coming back after supper? We will talk more then."

She nodded her head, and as soon as she was out the door I said to Rachel, "I want you to talk to Clara and see if we can use the living room tonight."

"Mom, why are you doing this to yourself? We need to find out a lot more about her. You can't just take her word that she is who she says she is."

"Rachel, don't argue with me. While you are at it, I want you to call as many of the family you can get hold of and ask them to come here this evening."

"Mom really.... And if I don't," Rachel said defiantly.

"Must you be this way every time I ask you to do something? If you don't want to, I will ask Clara."

I feel overwhelmed. Rachel is mad at me and stomping around, but I know this is something I need to do. I know this strange young lady is my great-granddaughter.

Four

Elyse was stunned by how easily she had given into the old woman demands. Yet, when she thought about meeting whoever "they" were, she realized this was going to be her one and only opportunity to let everyone know how she felt about how her grandfather was treated all these years.

Once again tears filled her eyes as she remembered him asking one final time "is she here yet?" It made her blood boil that not one person in his family cared enough to write a note or come to the funeral. Thinking he was dead was no excuse, *I am here aren't I? It had been easy to find them. As far as I know there are computers available for use in this area.*

Back at the Reindeer lodge she stopped at the restaurant, bought a large cup of black coffee, and went to her room. Taking her laptop out of the case and logging in, she checked her e-mail then opened her word processor. She typed a few brief sentences for her travel column. Opening another folder she wrote a detailed description of her encounter with Sarah and her feelings about the afternoon. *I'll have a lot more to add when I get back tonight.*

The bed beckoned her. She was tired from the long journey and felt emotionally spent and restless. Deciding against a nap she opted for a long warm bath. Surrounded by the warm water, with her head lying against the back of the tub she thought of the exact words she was going to tell "them." After finishing what she intended to say, she was going to make a dramatic exit leaving them a lot to think about. *I really don't give a damn what they think about me.*

With a start, she broke out of her reverie. She glanced at her watch lying on the vanity and suddenly realized she had slept for over an hour.

She got out of the tub, wrapped a towel around her and studied her face in the mirror. The piercings in her eyebrow and left side of her nose added character she thought. The tiny rose tattoo on her right wrist added the right touch.

Usually she wore no makeup other than black eyeliner, and that was because it drew attention to her deep blue eyes. Tonight she added a dash of lip gloss- her going out in company face. Dressing quickly in a pair of tight black jeans, too short white top and black stiletto heels she gathered her purse and car keys and ran out the door.

When she turned into the service road in front of the lodge, she was amazed to find it lined with cars and pickup trucks. It took her several minutes to find a parking spot, and she had to walk for a block to get to the front doors.

She breathed deeply then pulled one of the double doors open. *It's my turn finally. I'll tell them what I think and leave for home tomorrow.*

She felt uncomfortable walking into a room filled with strangers. She spotted Mrs. Walker, sitting on a sofa and, with a forced smile on her face, walked over to her. *These must be some of the other family member she was to meet.*

She actually felt like turning around and running from the room. *Who are all these people? Grandfather never mentioned having so many brothers and sisters. This is even worse than I thought. Why couldn't at least one of them have come before he died?*

Sarah saw the uncertainty on Elyse's face when she stepped into the room. She smiled, patted the empty seat beside her and reached out her hand. Elyse felt her face turn red. The room suddenly became quiet as everyone turned and watched her walk over to Sarah's side.

Sarah stood up and took her hand. She cleared her throat and then spoke as loudly as she could. "This is Elyse Walker, Ivan's granddaughter, my great-granddaughter."

Each person had a stunned look on their face. Although the room was filled with people Elyse instantly knew all were related to each other. In some way, each reminded her of her grandfather. Most of them had the same eyes and narrow forehead.

Turning to Elyse Sarah continued. "Ivan left home when he was fifteen. The younger ones have only heard about him, the older ones barely remember him."

"Mrs. Walker?"

"Call me gram, everybody else does."

"Who are all of these people? I don't understand."

"Why, these are some of Ivan's brothers and sisters, their wives, children, even a few great-grandchildren. They are all Rachel and I could get together this afternoon on such short notice. You will be able to meet the others at a later date."

"There are more?" Elyse blurted out.

"Yes, a few more." Sarah replied.

"Rachel, take Elyse and start introducing her to everyone. These are all family members she has never met."

Graciously Rachel led her to the first group of people. "This is my brother Joshua and his wife Betty. He was next to Ivan, only eighteen months apart." Elyse shook hands with both of them.

"Over here is another brother Jacob and his wife Linda, Jacob is a year younger that Joshua. Next to him is Samuel. His wife Carole is a nurse and couldn't come tonight. That is their son Todd and his wife Caroline over there."

Elyse smiled and shook hands with each, but her head was already spinning. *I don't know how I am going to remember all of these names and faces.*

Moving to another group Rachel said "this is my sister Anna. She was just a little over three pounds when she was born. Mom didn't know if she was going to make it, but she did. Our sister Helen, who was a year older than Anna, died of Whooping Cough when she was a baby."

Turning to the group behind them Rachel added, "This is my husband Tony holding our new granddaughter Sarah Jane. We named her after mom. Another brother, Peter, is flying in tomorrow. He runs his own business, Eagle Transport, maybe you have heard of it?"

"Can't say that I have," Elyse replied.

When Rachel finished introducing her to each person Elyse made her way back to where Sarah was sitting. "How many are there?" she asked.

"There were seven boys and three girls, including Helen. I have thirty two grandchildren and ten great-grandchildren, with more on the way.

Before she could say any more Rachel joined them. "Mom, why are you doing this? This person waltzes in here from out of the blue, tells you a big story and your believe her? For all we know she is going to rob you blind."

"Rachel, stop talking like that right now. Elyse, why don't you get something to eat, and then you can tell us all about Ivan."

As Elyse walked away Sarah turned to Rachel, "I know what I am doing. Contrary to what you might think, I still have most of my faculties. Leave me be, and please go get me a cup of tea."

"Mom, I'm going to ask her to leave."

"No, you are not," Sarah replied firmly.

Earlier the staff of the Lodge had brought in a cart filled with sandwiches, squares and the big coffee urn they used for special occasions. Elyse waited until everyone was lined up and then went to the back of the line. Rachel moved in behind her and said curtly "I don't know who you are or what you expect to accomplish. I, for one, am not going to let you walk in her and fill mom's head full of crap. I am her guardian- you have to get past me. You probably aren't even aware that she just turned ninety and has serious heart problems. Too much excitement isn't good for her."

Elyse bit her tongue. Although she was tempted to retaliate she didn't say anything.

For several seconds the two women stared at each other as the air bristled between them. Finally Elyse looked away. *This is neither the time nor the place to get into an argument.*

"Are you trying to tell me something?"

"Yes," Rachel replied acidly "don't upset her any more than you have."

This is becoming too much. I thought I would be here for an hour or so, say my piece and leave early in the morning. Now I am being threatened by that old battle axe and I haven't said anything yet.

When most had finished eating Sarah turned to Elyse and said. "Now my dear, tell us about Ivan."

"How do we know you are who you say you are?" Rachel demanded interrupting her mother.

Elyse was stunned by the animosity in her voice but before she could say anything Sarah spoke up.

"Rachel, for heaven's sake, let the child tell us her story. She has come a long ways to be here and besides she showed me a picture of Henry and me. I clearly remember the day it was taken" "See here it is." Sarah held up the picture for all to see.

"You don't know if I am telling the truth" Elise fired back angrily. "You will have to take my word that I am."

"Rachel, leave that poor girl alone. The rest of us want to hear what she has to say" said a male voice from the back of the room. "Go ahead Elyse, we all want to hear."

"According to what Grandfather told us," Elise recounted "he left home to work on a threshing crew that finished the season in Idaho. After leaving the threshing crew he drifted around the country picking up odd jobs where he could find them. By the sounds of what he told us, he lived a pretty rough life, never staying in one place long enough to settle down.

The day after Pearl Harbour was attacked he enlisted in the Navy. He felt he owed that much to the country that had been so good to him, but he turned out not to be much of a sailor. From there he transferred to the construction battalion, known as the Seabees. They built airstrips, bases, roads, pretty well anything that needed to be built in any arena of the war. Grandfather drove a bull dozer and was a mechanic. He was happier there doing what he loved.

After he finished boot camp training, he was sent to Alaska. Apparently the Japanese had captured two islands in the Aleutians, and his battalion was sent there in case they attempted to capture more land. They built a naval base which was later used to take those islands back.

From there he went to the pacific arena to fight and ended up in a place called Guadalcanal. His job was to help keep the landing strip open for the planes. Grandfather often told us about how they would get the runways fixed, then the Japanese would come, bomb them, and they would fix them again. He had a way of embellishing stories, so if you listened to him talk, you would think he did this single handed.

He was wounded several times; once in the arm, but the most serious was to his back in 1944. He was put on a hospital ship and ended up in Hawaii, where he stayed until the end of the war.

After he got back to the States he worked as a rough neck on oil rigs in Texas, California, Oklahoma, and finally ended up in Montana. He used to tell us he decided to stay there because that part of the country reminded him of home.

He met and married Grandma Iris, I think she was his second wife, but he never talked about the first. Together they bought a ranch, raised purebred Black Angus cows, and raised three children, Bobby, Joe and Billy. My dad is Bobby. I have two brothers, but I am the only granddaughter in the family.

We all lived on the ranch, but not in the same yard. Grandfather always wanted his family close by. "Don't want to lose any of you," he used to say. "This way I know where everyone is."

Grandfather hadn't been feeling good for a long time and my mother tried to talk him into going to the doctor. His excuse for not going was "I must have eaten something that didn't agree with me."

Finally the day came when the pain got so bad he went on his own. He was diagnosed with liver cancer, but had waited too long. The doctors told him there was nothing they could do. He was only in the hospital two weeks before he died."

Then she looked at Sarah, her eyes filled with tears, her shoulders tense. "He begged for you to come, to be with him. He wanted to see you one more time. He waited and hoped, but not one of you showed up. No notes, no phone calls, nothing from you."

By now the tears were running down her cheeks, "My grandfather was a good man, loud, and rough around the edges, but he would have given you the shirt off his back if you needed it. He didn't deserve to die alone waiting for family who cared less about him." She rubbed the tears from her eyes with her hands. *I don't want them to see me cry.*

The room was silent. Rachel reached over and put one hand protectively on her mother's hand. Unconsciously Sarah reached over and put her other hand on Elyse's arm.

"It's okay to be angry Elyse. We thought he was dead. After the war Henry and I waited for him to come home, but he never did. After a while we gave up waiting, but I never gave up hoping that one day he would knock on the door and walk in hollering like he used to.

Anna wrote to the United States Army in Washington, but we never got an answer. She has tried through her computer, but can't seem to find any information. The fact that you showed up here today is a miracle, and an answer to an old lady's prayers."

The uncomfortable silence of the room was shattered when someone said "who is up for one more game of Whist?" Everybody started talking at once. All of them acted as if nothing unusual had just taken place.

Elyse could see Mrs. Walker was getting tired, and the puzzled look on her face indicated that she was trying to make sense of all she had been told.

"Mrs. Walker, I'm leaving for home tomorrow. May I stop and see you before I leave? I have some pictures on my lap top I want to show you,"

"That will be fine dear. Come around ten," Sarah replied.

When people started to leave, Elyse quietly slipped out of the room and slowly walked back to her car. She was confused, her thoughts jumbled in her head. *I was prepared to hate these people for mistreating my grandfather, but there is nothing to hate. Was it possible I misunderstood the situation? If so, I have made a first class fool of myself in front of them.*

Once back in her room, she took off her jeans

and wrapped herself in the white terry bath robe hanging in the closet. Sitting in the dark, her head against the headboard of the bed and arms wrapped around her knees she tried to absorb all that taken place that day.

These are good people. Maybe what Mrs. Walker said was true, that sounded like something grandfather would do. He was a loner and hated the idea of reporting where he was going and what he was doing. Sometimes, when I think back, he would leave for weeks and nobody knew where he was. Grandma Iris always used to say she would start worrying when the police showed up at the door.

AUTHOR NAME

Five

Elyse lay for a long time but she couldn't fall asleep. She walked over to the desk, opened her lap top and began typing. She wrote for several hours, putting in as many details as she remembered about her evening with the Walker family, and her impressions of the individual family members. The fact she had excellent recall made her task that much easier.

When finished, she packed her laptop and suitcase, keeping out enough clothes out for the next day. Eventually she fell into a troubled sleep.

The next morning Elyse couldn't get finished packing fast enough. *I am out of here. I said what I came to say, but I might as well have stayed home. Not one single person, except maybe Mrs. Walker cares what I had to say. The rest could have cared less. I should just leave and not bother to say goodbye.*

At the front desk she turned in her key, paid for

the room and put her suitcase in the backseat of her blue mustang. She stopped at a service station, filled her car with gas, checked the oil and washed the windows. This car, which was her pride and joy, had been bought with her inheritance money from her grandfather. But, as she was driving out of town she saw the lodge and changed her mind. *At least Mrs. Walker has been half ways decent to me, not like that daughter of hers. I would hate to have to go through life being like her.*

She turned into the long driveway and parked in front of the entrance to the main lodge. Once inside, she walked briskly down the hallway, and stopped in front of room two twelve. Taking a deep breath she knocked. Right away she heard footsteps shuffling toward the door. She immediately saw how tired Mrs. Walker looked as she motioned Elyse to come in.

"I came to say good bye Mrs. Walker. I am packed, ready to go, but I wanted to give you my address and phone number before I left."

Mrs. Walker shuffled back across the room, sat down on the loveseat, and motioned for Elyse to sit beside her. "Forgive me for asking child but why did you come here? How did you find us? What is it you really want? You seem to be upset with us. Why? What can we do to make this better?"

Instead of sitting down Elyse walked over to the

window and stared out. Sarah could see that she was fighting to hold back her emotions. Suddenly Elyse burst into tears. All of her pent up feelings and emotions spilled out in a torrent of words.

"I have no history. I don't know where I belong, or who I belong to. Mom didn't have much family and dad would just say go ask your grandfather.

Mrs. Walker, my grandfather was a good man, and he died a lonely one. He used to tell me stories about living on the farm. When he called out for you I was mad that nobody was there for him."

Turning to look at Sarah she added, "I need to know what terrible thing he did that made you write him off this way, I came here with the intention of telling you what I thought of you and your family, and then leaving. Now I don't know what to think. I miss him so much."

Sarah sat listening, her hands neatly folded on her lap. Her mother always told her God gave us two ears and one mouth. This seemed like a good time to heed her advice.

"The day after his funeral," Elyse continued, "I was sorting through the box of pictures grandfather always kept in his dresser drawer. I found one of a man and woman standing side by side staring into the camera. The man was tall, dark haired and stern looking. He was dressed in bib overalls over a plaid shirt and looked a lot like grandfather. The woman, who barely reached his shoulders, was laughing. She wore a faded house dress and had bare feet. I could tell, from the picture she was happy.

Behind them were windows of a log house, and what appeared to be a back door. At one corner there was a covered barrel with a tin watering can on top. I remembered a story he used to tell about almost drowning in a rain barrel and wondered if it was the same one. On the back, barely legible were the words Sarah, Henry Walker and Clarion.

That night, out of curiosity, I typed the word Clarion into the search engine of my computer. Hundreds of names, most of them newspapers showed up, and I almost missed the one that said Clarion Alberta. Within minutes, I had a phone number."

"Really" said Sarah, "I didn't know you could do that. Why didn't you phone then, instead of driving up here?"

"I was curious. I wanted to see where grandfather came from, and who the two people in the picture were, so on an impulse I decided to come here.

I am a junior reporter for our local newspaper and convinced my boss to give me some time off. I promised I would write a travel column about our neighbours to the north. I took part of the rather large inheritance I got from grandfather, bought my dream car, a baby blue Mustang convertible and left home.

So, here I am." Elyse was still crying.

Gram let her cry until the storm passed.

"Elyse, do you really have to leave today? Can you stay a little longer?"

"I can stay if you want me to. I took a leave of absence from the newspaper, and I wasn't planning on going back to college until the second semester."

"Why don't you stay for a day or two, I have much I would like to share with you."

"I don't know. I will have to think about it. Right now I am not sure what would be the best thing to do."

Sarah began to panic. *I can't let her leave yet. I just found her. If she leaves now I will never see her again. Oh Lord, how did I not find him? I knew all along he was still alive, and I should have looked harder. This child is my only link to Ivan and the kind of a life he had. I don't have much time left. There must be a way I can convince her to stay a little longer.*

Sarah, once again, patted the seat beside her. "Come and sit for a while child."

Elyse was embarrassed and confused. Part of her was wishing she hadn't stopped and driven out of town, the other wanting to stay and learn more. They sat in companionable silence for a long time each lost in their own thoughts.

"Mrs. Walker I…"she started to say, but when

she looked over, she saw the old lady was asleep Picking the crocheted red and black granny square afghan off the back of a nearby chair she gently covered her. Then she kissed her on top of her head and let herself out the door, quietly closing it behind her.

After leaving the lodge, Elyse's first stop was back to the motel to see if she could get her room back for a few more days. Once she had all of her things moved back in she drove to the town's only office supply store and stocked up on paper, a cartridge for her printer, batteries and tapes for the recorder she always carried with her, photo paper, two steno notebooks and six pens. She had an idea. *If this doesn't work out I have enough supplies to last for a lifetime. There is a story here. I want to remember all of this.*

Returning to her room she set up an office area on the desk. Once satisfied, she drove to the Information Centre she noticed when she drove into town. There she picked up copies of all the available brochures on the town and surrounding areas. For the next several hours she walked through the museum, and made background notes on the local history. She also purchased a copy of the local history book because there was a whole chapter on the Walker family.

She spent the evening writing out an outline and

deciding what was the most important information she needed to find out. This would keep her on track, and when she was finished, she would have a complete history of the family written down. *I am sure my dad will find this interesting. Just think a whole family of uncles and cousins he didn't know a thing about.*

Six

The next morning when Elyse returned to Sarah's room, the older lady didn't seem surprised to see her. "Good," she said, "I was hoping you would decide to stay."

"Mrs. Walker I have an idea. I thought about this after I left yesterday. I am going to stay until Monday, and you can tell me more about our family. Perhaps it will help me understand what happened between you and my grandfather. If you don't mind, I thought I would write down the history as you tell me."

"Why on earth would you want to do that child?"

"I'm not sure why. I have a feeling I am in the right place at the right time. Not only will this make an interesting addition to my travel diary, but I can share it with the rest of my family. They are curious about grandfather too."

The Lord does provide. Yes, my child you have arrived just in time. I am not going to be here much longer.

"Elyse, if we are going to spend this much time together I have a few questions, and I want the truth."

Instantly Elyse became defensive. "Mrs. Walker, do you think I am making this up? Ivan Walker was my grandfather. I can prove it to you. My dad has more information. Wasn't that picture proof enough? What more do you want?" She turned to leave muttering under her breath,

"Maybe this wasn't such a good idea after all."

As she spoke Elyse's voice rose higher and higher. Tears filled her eyes as she picked up her purse and opened the door "I'm out of here. I can see why grandfather left and didn't come back."

"Elyse, come back here and sit down. We are not finished yet." Sarah commanded. "I know you are Ivan's granddaughter, knew it the minute I saw you. You have his eyes.

Rachel thinks you are here to scam me out of my life savings. I am telling you up front I will not give you one penny. I may be old, but I'm not stupid. If that is your intention you can leave right now, and this will be the end. This conversation will only be between the two of us, and nobody will be any wiser."

Elise was stunned. *What was with the old cow Rachel anyway?* Then it dawned on her. This visit could easily be misconstrued. She hadn't thought of that.

"Mrs. Walker?"

"Call me Gram, everybody else does."

"Gram, I wouldn't do that. I'm not that kind of a person."

"I happen to be pretty good judge of character Elyse and I know you are being truthful. For now let's keep what we are planning to do a secret. I have always wanted to leave a record my family history, but I don't have enough education. Your ability and my story make us a good team. When we are finished, we will give this story to Anna, and she can do what she wants with it."

Then, laughing out loud, Sarah continued "This will serve Rachel right. She doesn't trust anybody, most of all other women."

"I don't understand why you want to keep this a secret."

"That's easy. You haven't heard my stories before, so you will let me talk. The others don't listen any more. They say "Mom you have told us that story a dozen times already" and then change the subject."

"Sounds good to me Gram," Elyse replied in a conspiratorial tone. "My lips are sealed."

Thus began the morning ritual. The subject of Elyse leaving was never brought up again. Many evenings she worked late into the night to record what she was told. Then, each morning Elyse would read to Sarah what she had written the night before. Sometimes Sarah made a point clearer, other times she listened and said nothing. Elyse made the necessary changes in her laptop.

There were days Gram was busy or didn't feel well. On those days Elyse drove around the country side, taking pictures and writing her travel column.

Other times they spoke of different things. Elyse shared her hopes, dreams, and grandfather's stories with Sarah. Sometimes his stories had been so far-fetched they were hard to believe, but Sarah loved them anyway. The days of anger and mistrust were behind them. They bonded and became friends, each fulfilling the desire to know more about the other and about Ivan.

Seven

I am glad Elyse and I hit it off right from the beginning. We were comfortable with each other, and I like being round young people. Their lives are so much different than ours.

Once I got past Elyse's piercings, and her funny hair cut I found a warm, friendly, funny young lady who always seemed to be tense. At first she seemed to be all business, but that slowly changed as we got to know each other better. I also thought she had an attitude problem but I soon realized she was hurting. She must have loved Ivan very much.

* * *

"Mrs. Walker, Gram, start telling me your story and I will make a few notes. Don't worry about me getting it wrong, I have excellent recall. If I get something wrong you can correct me later. I brought my tape recorder. We can use that if you wish."

"No, I don't hold with all of the gadgets you young ones have today. Where do you want me to start?"

"Wherever you want to, how much can you remember?"

"There is nothing wrong with my mind young lady," she replied jokingly, "We will start at the beginning."

Elyse got a funny look on her face as if Sarah had reprimanded her. Then she smiled and teased Sarah back, "I guess that's as good a place as any. I should have thought of that."

"I was born in Odessa Russia. My father often told me the story about why his parents moved from Germany. They were promised a better life. He never did tell me why they were willing to move. Even now I wish that I asked more questions so I could have understood more.

A small group of Germans from his area were enticed to move to Russia, where they built small villages and were basically self-sufficient. They worked hard to build a new life, and many prospered and became quite wealthy and influential.

My dad's brother, Carl immigrated to Canada in nineteen hundred and loved his new country. He often wrote letters urging his family to move to this place of beauty and freedom. My parents wished him well, but were happy and content where they were.

As I understand it, the Russian peasants living in the area were illiterate, poor, and jealous of how prosperous the Germans had become. After the old Czar died, the new one, his son, began to strip away the rights his father promised the German immigrants. The first to go was the exemption from military service. Then, they moved an Administrator into the village as an overseer. The first thing he did was increase the taxes to the point people could no longer pay, and then he confiscated their property. I remember hearing my parents talk about what a cruel man he was and that most people were afraid of him.

Religion played an important part of the daily activities in the village, and one day he put out a proclamation declaring that the church was to be closed. The villagers were forbidden to go there to worship.

My father had five brothers, and one of them, Joseph, was the priest in our village. My father, who had a strong belief in God, openly defied the order by going to church every day as he always did. Some of the villagers, like my father, demanded the return of the rights they had been promised when their families agreed to move to Russia. Village officials warned him several times to keep quiet, but he was a stubborn man and openly defied every order the Administrator gave. My mother was always afraid something would happen to him.

I still remember clearly the day our life changed. I was playing on the swing he made me when I saw his cousin Berner's horse and buggy turn off the road and race into the yard. Berner jumped off and ran into the house. Within a few minutes, through the open window, I could hear him and my father arguing.

"Gus you have to listen to me, they are coming this way. The army has a list of names of those they consider traitors and your name is on it."

"How can that be? I am nothing but a lowly farmer going about my work. How am I making trouble for the army? The only one I make trouble for is that stupid man who is the village Administrator."

"I don't know how or why or who put your name on their list, but it is there... Maybe that's the reason; the Administrator wants to get rid of you. Yakov Britinsky saw the list, and he was the one who told me your name was there. He came to me first thing this morning and asked me to come tell you. You must leave as quickly as possible."

"I'm not leaving here. This is my land and my father's before me. I have worked hard to provide a decent life here for my family. If they come for me I will seek sanctuary in the church with my brother Joseph. They will not bother a priest."

"You know they have no respect for the church. That won't protect you, even the priests are considered to be traitors now. Certainly Joseph will be, considering he is your brother.

Please reconsider Gus. According to Yakov, they are going from village to village with their list arresting people. Some of those they denounce as traitors are shot on sight. Others are beaten, dragged away and disappear. Think of your family and what could happen to them."

After Cousin Berner left, I went into the house. "Mother, why were cousin Berner and father arguing?" I asked. "What does this mean? Is the army going to come and take father?"

"Shh little one, everything is fine, there is nothing to worry about, Now go and play while I finish making this bread. Heaven knows I have had more than enough interruptions today."

For the rest of the afternoon I heard my parents arguing about Berner's visit. My mother was upset and crying.

That night, during supper father announced "we are leaving tonight to go to Odessa to see my cousin Marie and her family. Put on two changes of clothes and your heavy coats because it will be cold in the night air. Gather the rest of your clothes, and your favourite toy, and Mother will pack them into a bundle for each of you. The rest of your things will be here when we return." Mother's eyes were red from crying and father was very abrupt.

While I was packing my clothes and helping my brothers with theirs, mother was busy packing our two wooden trunks. In the big one, the one that father's grandfather made, she put bread, butter, apples, potatoes, flour, biscuits, whatever she could find quickly. In the smaller one she put our family bible, the silver grandmother had given her, her jewelry and our important papers.

Mother was still trying very hard not to cry, and I was afraid. I knew this had something to do with Cousin Berner's visit earlier in the day. I thought we were going to Odessa and staying there until the soldiers forgot about my father, and when we returned home, all would be forgiven.

Father moved our horse and wagon to the back of the house and filled the box with clean straw. He loaded the two trunks across the back, and near the front mother made us a bed in the straw. Just before we left, Father opened the gate to the yard to let the cow out, and left the door of the chicken coop open. I knew then we wouldn't be back for a long time.

I was seven years old. My older brother Gus was nine and my little brother Adolph was two, almost three. The night was very dark with barely enough moonlight for the horses to see their way. We stayed on the main road and, when we passed the neighboring villages, I could hear their dogs barking. Sometimes I heard wolves howling in the distance. At first my brothers and I played in the straw each of us trying to get the best spot and making a lot of noise.

"Children," mother told us," you must be very quiet. We don't want to wake anyone up. They have to get up early and go to work in their fields."

We didn't know that sound carries in the night, and my parents didn't want anyone to hear us. My mother kept whispering to my father that she was afraid, but he kept reassuring her that everything would be all right.

When we complained of being hungry, mother gave us each a biscuit, an apple and drink of water from the jug she had brought with her. Soon my brothers fell asleep, but I laid awake for a long time listening to my parents talk quietly to each other.

Father drove all night, and as the sun began to come up, he turned off the road and followed a well-used path into the forest. We followed this path for a short time, and then he stopped. By now the sun was hot, but I still remember how cool it was under the trees. We sat there and waited. Finally we heard a whistle, and father's cousin Joe came out from among the trees. He and my father talked for several minutes, and I saw father give him some money. I was surprised because I knew he had been saving this money for a long time.

Father unhitched the horse, and then he and Joe pushed the wagon under some low hanging branches where nobody could see it. We left everything except the big wooden chest. Mother refused to leave it behind. She wanted to bring the smaller one too but father said no. Quickly she handed Gus and me our bundle of clothes to carry. Father carried the wooden chest on his shoulder; mother carried their clothes bundle and little Adolph's. I remember my bundle was very heavy. Before we left, she moved the family bible, her silver and jewellery and papers into the larger chest, and then we walked away.

We followed Joe through the trees for a long time. He kept telling us to be very quiet and made us keep walking when we wanted to rest. Other times, he made us stop while he disappeared into the trees. We sat and waited for him to come back.

At first my brothers and I thought we were having an adventure, but now we were getting scared. I held little Adolph's hand most of the time so he wouldn't be so frightened. Joe told us there were soldiers in the forest, and that we had to watch for them, but we didn't see any. I think they were being quiet too.

The last time we stopped father took me aside and whispered to me. "Sarah, I need you to be very brave. We are close to the border and to the soldiers. They must not find out we are here. I am going to have to leave you here alone for a time. Don't move or make any noise, and don't wander away. If you become afraid, pray to the Virgin Mary. If the soldiers find you, tell that them you wandered away and got lost in the forest. You are a child, they will believe you. Tell them to take you to the closest priest. You will be safe there. Don't tell them where you are from or your last name. Joe has somebody in the village watching for us if there is a problem. Stay here until Joe comes back for you. I promise he will come for you, but I'm not sure exactly when."

He kissed me on my cheek. Mother gave me two biscuits and an apple to eat. She was crying as they walked away. I knew she didn't want to leave, but father was pulling her by the arm. I waved at her to let her know I would be fine. Later, I found out that they left my brother Gus the same way, but in a different place. I wish we had been together.

I waited there the rest of that day and all that night. When I was frightened, I prayed just like Father told me to. It seemed to help. I remember looking up and trying to count all of the stars in the sky, but there were too many. Sometimes I heard noises in the woods, but none close to me. I played with my doll, divided the biscuits into four and ate each piece slowly. I slept a little.

Suddenly, as the sun was rising, I heard rustling in the trees and began to cry. I was sure the soldiers had found me, were going to take me away and kill me like they did the others. Then I heard someone softly calling my name. It was Joe. He finally came for me just like my father promised.

"Don't cry little one," he said "soon you will be safe with your parents."

I took his hand and we walked for a long time. Eventually, he lifted me over a wooden rail fence, and we ran into the forest on the other side. My mother, father and brothers were waiting for me. I was very happy to see them.

After Joe left, my father knelt down and put his arms around me. "You were a brave girl Sarah I am very proud of you. Joe couldn't come back for you sooner because the army was camped not too far away. He had to wait until they left before he could safely climb over the fence. We are in Germany now and safe. Come, we must leave before we are seen."

"I did like you told me to. I stayed in one spot."

He squeezed my shoulder and then picked up the big trunk. Mom carried Adolph, who was sleeping, and Gus and I walked behind. We followed a narrow path through the trees until we came to a road and then followed it. Just before dusk we came to a village. We walked until we found the church, and the priest took us in. Later I learned we were not the first he helped in this way. Many others were also fleeing the country. The town folks helped feed us and father did odd jobs in return.

Somehow, father got word to Uncle Carl and he sent us money for tickets on a ship that was coming to Canada. We took the train to a city called Bremen to a city called Bremen and boarded the ship there.

Eight

While we rode on the train to Bremen, I asked father why his parents moved from Germany. He explained to me that my grandparents, along with many others, moved to Russia from Germany in search of a better life. The immigrants were promised their own schools, freedom of religion, and freedom from military duty, and could continue to speak their own language. In exchange, they would cultivate and develop the farm land in the area. Over time, they became prosperous and influential.

They lived in small villages and grew apples, oranges, vegetables, grain and eventually their own vine yards. Every day the men and women left to work in the fields.

The Russian peasants living in the area were mostly illiterate and very poor. Over time they became jealous of the Germans becoming rich, and their conditions not improving. They complained, and slowly the new Czar began taking away the rights his father had promised the Germans. Unrest was building in the country, so the first to go was the exemption from military service. Then a Russian Administrator was brought in to take control of the village and the schools. He was a very cruel man who demanded and got the best of everything produced in the village. He treated the women badly and the men were afraid to stand up against him, in case they were punished. After increasing the taxes to the point that people could no longer pay he forbade the practice of religion and closed the church.

My father, who had a strong belief in the word of God, openly defied the order by going to church every day. He argued for farmer's rights and demanded the Administrator be removed and the village be allowed to return to the old ways. Naturally, this made him very unpopular with the Russians. They came to our house several times to warn him, and ordered him to stop talking and obey the rules, but he defied them and continued to resist every order given. That is probably why his name was on that list of troublemakers.

I remember feeling sorry for him. Now I realize how hard it must have been to walk away from everyone and everything he held dear. Even worse was that we had to sneak away in the dark of the night without having a chance to say goodbye to his friends and other family members.

I don't remember much about our arrival in Bremen. I do recall that the city was noisy and smelly. There was much confusion as the people got off the train, and we waited at the station with mother, while Father went to find the shipyards to buy our tickets.

We stayed overnight in a room near the harbor which was filthy, and smelled of fish and sweat. Mother spread a blanket on top of the bed, and we all slept on it. She was afraid there might be lice or bed bugs under the covers.

The next morning, we stood in line for hours, waiting for our turn to get on the ship. We were one family of many. I remember the shouting and confusion as others tried to push ahead. Mother and father stood quietly, Gus and I played tag with some of the other children.

We wondered what kind of a room we would have, but when it was our turn we were directed down into the bottom of the ship. There was little light, and all the people down there were crowded into one big open space. I remember the sound of children crying, and that it was very hot and stuffy.

Father found the sleeping area we were allotted, and was upset that it consisted of two bunks. There was no privacy. He thought that we would have a room, not herded into one space like cattle. Gus and

I slept on the top bunk, while mother, father and Adolph slept on the bottom. The big wooden chest sat on our bunk by our feet.

I don't remember much about our journey. I got sick on the second day from the rocking of the ship. Mother coaxed me to eat something and drink water, but as soon as I did, my food came back up.

We took turns going up onto the deck for fresh air, because mother was afraid someone would steal our food. There was a bad storm and I remember people crying and praying. If the ship sank we were afraid we would drown. We knew that many of us would be trapped, unable to get out.

More people got sick after that, including little Adolph. Mother sat on the side of the bunk holding and rocking him, trying to get him to drink a little water. She kept wiping his face with a damp cloth because he was burning up with fever. I will never forget the smell of so many sick people. Some people thought the sickness came because the water was bad, I never did understand the cause.

On the third day he died in mother's arms. She wrapped his little body in her white wedding shawl, and the captain buried him at sea. I remember standing there watching as his little body slipped into the ocean. This scene was repeated many times over the course of our journey as more children and the elderly died.

I can still see my mother sitting on the edge of her bunk, rocking back and forth crying, and the other women comforting her. My father was very quiet and sad. I didn't see him cry, but his eyes were red and puffy. He was also worried because we were running out of food. The storm forced us off course and the crossing took much longer than expected.

The second day after Adolph died he sat down beside mother. He put his arm around her and said, "I am sorry I have taken you away from your friends and family. We must move on from here. It's God's will that Adolph was taken from us, but we have to keep on living. If we don't, his life will be wasted because we gave up."

I don't remember her smiling or laughing for a long time after that, she always seemed to be sad. I think she missed Adolph and our home very much. After Adolph died I stayed with mother to look after her. I was afraid she would die too.

Uncle Carl was waiting for us when we got off the ship in Montreal. I still remember how good and clean the air smelled. From there we boarded a train and travelled to his home in Ontario where we stayed for the winter.

Father got a job, cutting logs into firewood, and then delivering the chopped wood to people's homes. By spring he saved enough for us to get back on the train. We travelled for three days and nights before we arrived at Alton, a small town in southern Alberta. Some of my mother's relatives lived there and they took us in.

By the time winter came father had built our own wooden frame house. It was very small, but I remember it had a wooden roof and floor. Maybe that was why having a roof and floor was so important when we moved north.

My four brothers and sisters were all born there. Gus and I always knew when a new baby was coming because father made the house a little bigger. It was a fair size by the time he finished.

I don't think my mom ever got over losing little Adolph. Even years later, her eyes filled with tears whenever she spoke of him. After my baby girl Helen passed away I understood how she felt. How her heart must have hurt.

There were many people in Alton who came from our area of Russia, and more moved there when they came to Canada. Later we found out that cousin Joe had been caught, tortured and hanged for smuggling people across the border. The army had come for my father the day after we left. When they couldn't find him, they tortured his brother Joseph for information, and then hanged him in front of the church. Mother and father hadn't told anyone of their plans to leave, and because of this, father always blamed himself for Joseph's death. Later we heard the rest of the community was driven from their homes and forced to move to the camps in Siberia. The peasants took over the farms and village."

Elyse was fascinated with the story she was being told. "I can't imagine going through such an ordeal as that. Were you scared? I know I would have been terrified?"

"Remember Elyse, I was only seven years old. I trusted my father. If he said Joe was coming back I knew he would. If Joe didn't, then my father would have come back for me, he wouldn't leave me there."

"But Gram, what if nobody had come?"

"To be honest I don't know if that thought ever crossed my mind."

Nine

Elyse noticed a framed picture of a young couple sitting upon the old antique round table at the end of the loveseat. She picked it up and studied it for several seconds. The man stood ramrod straight and was wearing a black suit and tie. Beside him was a young woman in a lace wedding dress and veil. Neither one were smiling.

"Is this you and Mr. Walker?" she asked.

"Yes, that's our wedding picture."

"How long were you married Gram?"

"Fifty five years when my Henry passed."

"Wow, that's a long time to live with one person. How old are you in this picture."

"I was eighteen, Henry was twenty one."

"How did the two of you meet?"

Sarah giggled like a school girl. "The first time I saw Henry Walker he was standing at the back of the church with his brothers, and I was in the choir. Everybody in town knew about the Walker boys and some of the things they did. They didn't have a very good reputation in the community. One or the other always seemed to be in trouble.

After church, while I was helping my mother

make supper, I asked, "How many Walker boys are there? Who was that with them this morning? I don't remember seeing him around here before."

"That was Henry," she replied. "He works away from home most of the time, but comes back in the spring and fall to help his brothers put the crop in."

"Ingrid told me they were all bad boys."

"I don't think they are bad, just a rough and tumble bunch of boys. They like to pull jokes on people. Sometimes they drink too much, and get into fights at dances. I would say they are more mischievous than bad.

Their father died when they were young, and those boys were a handful for their mother to raise, but I will say one thing for them. When they are home, they are in church every Sunday morning, no matter what they did the night before."

"I was a school girl, barely fifteen, and having only seen Henry that one time I developed a crush on him. He was tall and handsome with black wavy hair and the most beautiful deep blue eyes. They lived on a farm six miles west of Alton, and our family farm was five miles east and then north three miles.

Two years later, in the fall, Henry and his brother Jack came to help dad with the harvest. During the summer he had fallen from the loft of the barn and broke his leg, and my brothers were too small to take the crop off. That's what neighbors did when there was trouble. They helped each other.

Mom sent me out to the fields with lunch for the workers and on the second day Henry and I started talking. When they were finished I was sorry to see him leave. Come spring he dropped by to see if dad needed any help. After that he kept coming around on a regular basis. He pretended to see if my dad still needed help, but we both knew he was courting me.

One day he said to me "I am going to ask your dad if we can get married. Stay here and wait for me."

That's how things were done in those days. The boy had to make his intentions known to the girl's father.

Dad was in the back yard chopping wood. Henry walked back there, picked up an axe and began helping him. They chopped and talked for a long time, and then Henry came back with a dejected look on his face.

"Your dad thinks I am too wild and too old for you. He didn't say no, he just said he would have to think about it. He said I would have to settle down a lot first."

"I didn't know what to think. I was upset with my father and wanted to argue with him, but that would only make him more determined to say no. He could be a very stubborn man when he wanted to be. We were young, in love and angry because dad put a stop to our plans.

"What did you do then Gram?" Elyse asked.

"There wasn't much I could do but hope that my father would change his mind. Henry went away to work, and I waited for him.

That night I pleaded with my mother. "You don't know him like I do. He likes to have fun, but he works hard too, He sounds gruff and loud, but underneath he is a gentle soul. He would never hurt me."

Mom must have talked father into allowing us to get married because late the next spring he said we could after the harvest was finished. The priest was coming for only one church service in November so we decided that November 2, 1923 was as good a day as any.

The good weather held late that fall. There was no snow, but the air was crisp. There was only my family and his family at the church, probably about thirty of us in total. The priest rambled on and on and I thought he was never going to quit talking, I could also see that Henry was getting fidgety.

After the ceremony Allan Brownlea, a close friend of Henry's, drove us from the church to the farm, in his model T Ford, horn blaring all the way. Every once in a while he would pass a bottle back to Henry and they would have a wedding drink. I kept telling Henry to take it easy and not to drink too much. I didn't want him getting drunk before the reception. I also didn't want my father to think he had made a mistake.

Mom and the neighbour ladies cooked for days. Our two story house was small and would barely hold that many people at one time. The neighbours came later after their chores were done. Most of them stayed and partied all night.

What a party we had. The food was unbelievable, ham, fried chicken, traditional German dishes, salads, pie, cake and, of course, homemade beer and whiskey. George Brown brought his violin, Gordon Jones his guitar and Dwayne Allen his saxophone. We danced all night. When the little ones fell asleep their parents laid them in a row on the bedroom floor. After having a nip or two I think some of the older boys went to sleep there too.

Henry's brothers had him off in a corner, toasting his marriage with glasses of whiskey. Next thing I knew he was sitting with his back against the wall, his long legs splayed out in front of him - passed out. I left him there, then after a while I went upstairs and went to bed. I never dreamed I would spend my wedding night alone. Contrary to what you young people think we knew what sex was too, and Henry was getting quite persistent."

"Too much information Gram," Elyse said, her

face turning a delicate shade of pink.

He felt terrible the next morning and kept apologizing. His brothers had a good laugh at his expense. I couldn't stay angry, but throughout the years I teased him about his brothers pulling a   fast one on him.

The next day dad loaded the two us and our wedding gifts into his wagon and drove across country to our new home. We moved onto his mother's farm. We didn't have much of a house, a one room granary that Henry had fixed up, and it had a real roof. He had put in two small windows and a wooden door with a window in it. He also bought a Blackwood stove which took up most of one wall which we used for cooking and heating. Mom and dad gave us an old table, two chairs and a metal bed frame. Henry's mother made us a straw mattress and a wedding ring quilt.

We also got a set of everyday dishes, hand sewn tea towels and a silver tea set from Mrs. Gordon as wedding gifts. .I treasured that set and used it every time company came. Mother made us a set of bed linens with our initials embroidered on them. After Henry's brother passed around his boot at the reception we got fifteen dollars. We thought we were rich. If I remember correctly, we used the money to buy coffee, flour, sugar, tea and two cooking pots. After the ceremony the priest blessed and gave us our marriage cross. That's it hanging on the wall over there.

Henry made up for being drunk on our wedding night. That night he made me feel special and loved and I have never forgotten that feeling."

"TMI gram, too much information," Elyse said. They both laughed, Sarah's face was turning red from the recollection.

"Wait until you get married Elyse, you will see what I mean." Now, it was Elyse's' turn to be embarrassed.

"Where was I? Ivan was born the next fall, and the following spring we added two bedrooms to the house. Joshua was born in the early spring of the next year. We were like my parents, every time a new baby came we added onto the house.

My Henry was a good man; big, loud and full of pranks, but the children and I always came first. He was good to me and I still miss him very much.

We made a good team Henry and I. Times were tough, but somehow we always got through them. I remember, throughout our marriage, we often lay in bed talking until early morning. That is when we shared our hopes and dreams.

Henry wanted a farm of his own. He wanted a place where he could stand outside in the yard and see what he had accomplished with his own hands. He wanted to leave a legacy for our children.

We didn't fight much but when we did, they were real doozies. We were both of the same temperament, and didn't stay mad for very long. We both knew life was too precious to waste fighting. Although now, when I look back, I am sure that I got pregnant after every big argument we had. Making up was always the best part.

"Gram…" Sarah laughed at the expression on Elyse's red face.

"In the end Henry's and my dreams did come true. We built a good Christian marriage and life for our family. My only regret was moving so far away from my parents, brothers and sisters. There were a few visits but they were never long enough. If there was one thing I would have changed it would have been that. Family is important, don't ever forget that.

Ten

Elyse was composing a story on her lap top to send back to her editor when someone knocked on her door. *Who can that be* she wondered as she opened it and was surprised to see Rachel standing in the hall way. Before she could say anything, Rachel pushed her way into the room and slammed the door behind her.

"What do you think you are doing?" Elyse asked. "Better still, what do you want? Has something happened to Gram?"

"Young lady, I want you to pack up your things and leave today," Rachel spit out, " in fact I am here to help you along your way."

Instantly Elyse was angry. "Just who do you think you are coming into my room and telling me what to do?"

"I am sick of listening to mom say "Elyse this, Elyse that, Elyse says .... " I know what you are doing," Rachel said pushing her finger into Elyse's chest. "You are trying to get into her good graces, and then scam her out of everything she has. Well, I have news for you missy, she doesn't have anything left. She gave it all away when she sold her house."

By now Rachel was shouting. "You are wasting your time. Go now before you completely break her heart."

Elyse let Rachel ramble on for several seconds and then interrupted her tirade. "I don't know what you are talking about. What did you do, make up this little fantasy in your head? You have this all wrong.

Your mother isn't as old and senile as you want to believe. Her mind is as sharp as a tack. Besides she and I have already discussed this and have an understanding. I am who I say I am – Ivan's granddaughter and her great-granddaughter."

"And she believes your story?" Rachel replied sarcastically.

"Why not, it's the truth."

Rachel stopped shouting and looked Elyse over from head to toe. "I don't believe one word coming out of your mouth, but, unfortunately, I can't prove you are lying."

Elyse sighed. "Rachel I am telling you the truth. I have asked Gram for nothing except her time and she has given me nothing. That is our agreement. Have you even thought about how much this is costing me to stay here?"

"Then do yourself a favor and go home." Rachel said. "That way you will save yourself some money. We didn't ask you to come here and disrupt our lives."

She stepped back and opened the motel room door. "If

I find out otherwise I will have you arrested so fast your head will spin. Think about that young lady."

With that remark she flounced out of the room and down the hallway. Elyse watched her until she got to the end of the hall and then closed the door.

Just who does she think she is, coming here and accusing me of heaven knows what? I am so angry. What I should do is follow her and give her a piece of my mind.

She paced back and forth in her room muttering to herself until she began to calm down. *I can see where Rachel is coming from. What I don't understand is why she is so upset? Why doesn't she trust me? I haven't done anything to her.*

Still seething with anger Rachel drove from the motel to the lodge to see her mother. She knocked once on Sarah's door and then barged in. Sarah saw immediately that Rachel was upset.

"I just came from Elyse's room and told her to leave. In fact, I offered to help her pack," Rachel said.

"Why would you do that?" Sarah asked. "She isn't doing anything wrong; in fact I think coming here has been good for her. She and Ivan were very close and she is hurting. Besides, I am enjoying having her here."

"Trust you mom- always looking for the good in people. How much money has she asked you for, and how much have you given her?"

"Is that what you think this is that she is here to scam me?" Sarah replied.

"Well isn't she? Answer my question mom, how much have you given her so far?"

"Rachel, you have this all wrong. I know you are trying to protect me, but you don't have to worry. I haven't given her anything."

"How much has she asked you for then?"

Sarah ignored her question. "When Elyse arrived she was angry and confused, and rightly so. She was upset because her grandfather died and nobody from his family had been to see him. Now she is relieved to know we looked for him for years, and that she has found part of her family she didn't know existed. Our questions are being answered."

I am also grateful I found out Ivan had a good life I am asking you to let up on her from now on. It's not what you think; besides this is my business and none of yours,"

"You believe her. Why?"

"Simply because she hasn't given me any reason not to. Rachel I can still think for myself and am quite capable of making my own decisions. From now on you are going to keep what you think is going between Elyse and me to yourself. I don't need you running to other family members with this far-fetched story. Keep our opinion to yourself. There is nothing for you to be concerned about, and furthermore, we are not going to discuss this again - do you understand?"

Rachel started to argue back but when she got 'that look' from Sarah she stopped "I'll be keeping an eye on her."

"You do what you think you have to." Sarah replied. "Now it's nearly lunch time, walk down the hall with me and forget all of this foolishness. There is nothing for you to be concerned about."

Eleven

Elyse decided to stay at Clarion for several more weeks. She thought that would give her enough time to hear Mrs. Walker's story and still get back to work on time. On the desk in her motel room the pile of paper continued to grow

The next morning, when she arrived at the lodge, Gram wasn't in her room. She stopped to ask one of the employees "do you happen to know where Mrs. Walker is? She isn't answering her door."

"She is probably in the solarium. She goes there every morning – down at the end of the hall you can't miss it."

Elyse walked down to the end of the hall. Gram was there, sitting in a green paisley chair, with a black nylon bag at her feet.

Tentatively she asked "Gram, are you awake?"

"Just resting my eyes Elyse, I was waiting for you. I love this room. I can look out and see the fields and the trees, kind of reminds me of the farm."

"If you are too tired, I don't need to stay this morning."

"Nonsense child, I can talk just as easily here as I can in my room. Come and sit down and move your chair closer so we don't have to shout. Where were we? Yes, I told you about my move to Alton, but I think I should tell you how Henry got there.

Henry's family originally came from the same area as ours, but left in 1898 by ship and landed in the United States - Minnesota I think. Later they moved to North Dakota where Henry was born in 1900. With the promise of a better future they moved to Alton around 1910 I think but I'm not sure. I don't remember the exact dates any more.

His dad died when he was quite young and his mother had quite a time with all those boys. I'm not sure how they didn't drive her crazy, they were quite a handful.

 "Mom, there you are," Rachel exclaimed as she came bustling into the room. The sound of Rachel's loud demanding voice grated on Elyse's nerves.

"I thought I would find you here when you weren't in your room."

"Good morning Rachel," Sarah answered and then, with a hint of sarcasm, added, "good to see you too."

Then Rachel noticed Elyse sitting there. "I thought you home," she said acidly to Elyse. "What are you still hanging around for?" The animosity between the two women bristled in the air.

"I decided to stay for a few days, what's it to you?" The two women glared at each other.

Finally Rachel broke the silence. "You might as

well pack up and leave today. I am going to tell them at the front office that you aren't allowed in here anymore."

"Rachel, that is enough," Sarah spoke up, "Elyse is here because I asked her to stay."

Rachel turned on her mother, "now why would you do something like that? We all know she is here to see what she can get out of you."

"Enough," Sarah replied, "Stop acting like a spoiled child. You can either leave or join us, it's up to you."

Rachel turned and stormed out of the room. Elyse watched her leave. "I don't want to cause any trouble between the two of you Gram."

"Don't worry about her. That's just how Rachel is. She likes to be in control of everything. If it's not her idea she gets this way. Now where were we?

We continued living on the farm by Alton. Henry farmed with his brothers and they built a small herd of cattle. They had ten head and were hoping to keep more at calving time. They still had their moments. If they got together after having a few drinks a person was never quite sure what was going to happen.

Two more boys added to our blessings. We were both close to our families, and had many friends. At the time we didn't realize how lucky we were.

Then the wind began to blow, drying out the land,

leaving large cracks in the earth. What little rain we had was sucked up by the wind. We had no money and four little boys, Ivan, Joshua, Jacob and Mathew to think about. In the spring of 1933, Henry planted three hundred acres of wheat and harvested three hundred bushels, barely getting his seed back.

We sacrificed everything we had to pay our bills and keep food on the table. One at a time our neighbours lost their trucks and farm implements because they didn't have the money to finish paying for them. We traded hogs with each other for food. I give you a hog today so you can eat, and in return you give me one back from your next litter.

The gardens and prairie grasses dried up so, in the end, we had to butcher the animals because we didn't want them to starve. Prices were so low that if we had shipped them it would have cost us money. We did manage to keep one cow and a few chickens, so at least we had milk and eggs. There was no money to buy supplies like tea and coffee, and soon there was none to buy anyway.

Because Alton was on the rail line there were always men knocking on the door, looking for work or food. They travelled the country side doing whatever they could. When they came to my door, I did the best I could to help them, but after a while I had to turn them away. I had barely enough for own family. Now, when I think back I still feel guilty. I wish I could have done more.

We could have applied for government relief, but Henry was too proud for that. Those who did got a check for seven dollars a month during the winter to buy food for their families. In the summer time, they paid it back by working on the roads for the government.

"How did you end up here Gram? It must have been hard packing everything you had and moving here?"

"I didn't have much choice Elyse. As usual this was one of Henry's ideas. I was against moving, but in the end, it turned out to be a good thing.

At the time the government was offering free rail transportation to anyone willing to move north to the Peace country. Henry, his brother Joe, and a neighbour George Adams decided to go to Peace River to find how things actually were. They didn't exactly trust the government.

They returned with stories of good crops, open land casy to rent, big trees and lots of water. When he got back Henry applied to homestead two quarters of land. He could get one and I could get another.

The next spring, we packed all of our belongings, loaded them on the train and left the prairies. Henry's mother and all of his brothers, except William and one sister, followed us one month later. We all settled in the Cross Roads area.

It took us three days and two nights by train to reach Clarion, which was probably the longest three days of my life. Henry and Ivan rode in the box car with the cow, two new horses and our other belongings, the other boys and I rode in a coach. We couldn't afford to buy a sleeper for the nights, so I sat up and slept, and the boys stretched out on the seats.

I packed a big lunch for us, bread, apples, sausage, cheese, things that would keep. When the train stopped to pick up other passengers I took food and water back to Henry and the cattle.

After the first hour the boys were bored from being confined and kept running up and down the aisle annoying the other passengers. It was all I could do to keep from pulling my hair out. When the train stopped for longer periods of time to take on coal and water I took them outside to run off their energy. At every stop there were people selling food, but I couldn't afford to buy any.

We arrived at Clarion early in the morning. The boys and I waited in the station until Henry had everything unloaded. By then it was getting late so he got us a hotel room and he stayed with the wagon and animals. I remember the room cost two dollars, and after being on the train for so long it felt like heaven to have a bath and sleep in a real bed.

The next morning as soon as the store opened I

bought some supplies to take with us. Henry took us to the café for breakfast, and then stopped to get directions to our place and we headed out to our new home. We didn't have much money with us and being in town had already cost more than we expected. Henry arranged to store our equipment until we could come and pick it up. We figure we would need the money to pay for that. When we did, there was no charge and the fellow eve helped us move it to the farm.

After that it took the rest of that day and most of the next by horse and wagon to get to our farm. The boys and I took turns riding in the wagon, Henry walked beside. We had all our belongings in there and Daisy, our milk cow was tied behind. The roads were muddy and flooded in some places.

That first night we camped at a dry spot along the road with the stars as our roof. The mosquitos, which were huge, kept us swatting most of the night. We arrived, tired and dirty, at our new home the middle of the next afternoon.

When I saw the shack we were to live in, I told Henry, "I am not living in that pig sty. It is too small, made of logs, and is most likely full of mice and other critters." I wanted to go back to my comfortable home and my family.

The house was twelve by twenty feet and consisted of two rooms. One we used as a kitchen and living area, the other I partitioned off for two bedrooms. Henry and I shared one, the boys the other. There wasn't a lot of privacy in those days. The biffy was outside behind the house.

Henry went inside and then came out. "Now, now, mama, look it has shingles on the roof and a plank floor. There is even glass in one of the windows. We will be just fine. I can easily put the door back on its hinges and a good scrubbing will make a big difference."

"Why was it so important to you to have a wooden roof and floor Gram? Didn't all houses come that way?" Elyse asked.

"On the prairies some of the homes had sod roofs and every time it rained the water dripped inside for another day. If there was a dirt floor I never would have been able to keep my house clean. If I had both, I would be living in mud all the time."

Elyse giggled. "I see your point now."

"When I looked inside, all I could see was a dirty black cook stove in one corner and cob webs hanging from the rafters. He was right about one thing; at least it didn't have a dirt floor.

We camped outside that first night, and then all of us pitched and cleaned the place up. I absolutely refused to sleep inside until it was clean, and I was sure there were no mice. It was a long time before I forgave him for not finding land with a better house.

The next morning I found what used to be a garden spot, and immediately started digging the weeds out. I wanted to get the seeds I had brought with me into the ground, hoping some would produce by fall. Mostly I planted potatoes. There was a spring nearby so we had lots of fresh water for us and the cattle. Henry made me some shelves by the stove to put the pots and pans and dishes on.

Good thing Daisy was a good miller. After the boys had drank their fill every day I made butter and cottage cheese from the rest. I wrapped it tightly in oil cloth and stored the packages in the crock I dug into the bank of the spring. The water was cold which kept them from spoiling. Later on, after I got my chickens, I traded the butter and eggs at the General store for things we needed like sugar, coffee and flour.

When the roads dried up and we were settled Henry went to town to get our machinery. I asked him to take some of the butter with him to see if he could trade it for something. He came back with three laying hens, a rooster and a small keg of nails. We used the nails to build a log framed black smith shop and a lean to for the cattle. I don't recall why but, we ended up naming our new place the Homestead.

Soon the neighbours were bringing their plough shears over for sharpening. The boys would help

Henry by turning the crank on the blower for air to keep the fire good and hot. I can still see him standing there, the sweat running down his face and dripping off his chin.

One of the first things I noticed was how long the days were. There was quite a difference between here and down south. In the winter it was dark most of the time. There were only a few hours of daylight we could use to get the chores done. That was even harder to get used to.

"How were you able to sleep, going to bed in the daylight and getting up in the daylight. I know I would have had trouble," asked Elyse.

"Most of the time we were too tired to care. For me, the best time of the day was the early morning – listening to the birds sing, the leaves rustle in the trees. By evening there were so many bugs it was hard to stay outside. Henry kept a smudge going day and night to help the animals. We felt like we had so much to do and not enough time.

Henry was told winters could be very harsh, as much as forty degrees below zero. We honestly didn't know what to expect. The winters down south never got that cold. At first, we thought the neighbours were teasing us, but they were right. It was a good thing the cabin was small and easy to heat.

Our first winter was hard. The temperature

dropped to more than forty below zero and stayed there for the whole month of January. On the prairies, after a few cold days, a chinook would blow in and warm things up, but not here. Henry used what straw we had as bedding for the cows and chickens. One big difference was that we didn't get blizzards like we did back home.

My Henry was a shrewd trader. Many times he traded his work for things we needed, like seed, grain, or potatoes. Whatever was offered, he took. If he couldn't use what he got, he traded that with the next fellow that came along.

Sometimes when the men came, they brought their wives. I was always hungry for female company. Often the women brought a jar of jam or honey as a gift, which I stored in a wooden box by the stove for us to use in the winter. While the men were outside, we would have tea and they would share ideas about how to make our lives more comfortable. I got a lot of good tips from them. Their kids played outside with ours.

That first summer, before we got what little crop we had harvested, we ran out of flour and had neither money nor credit to get any more. Late one night there was a knock at the door and one of our neighbours, Bill Parsons, brought us a sack of flour. Henry was to return it in the fall after we got our crop came off.

Henry was a proud man, and it was hard for him to accept charity. The first thing he did was pay back that sack of flour in the same way he received it. That way nobody knew what had taken place except them. To this day I don't know how Bill found out we needed that flour. Bill never said and Henry never asked. Without his kindness, I don't know how we would have survived.

Henry and the boys cleared the land with an axe leaving the big trees in the fields. In the fall the neighbours took turns helping each other move the fallen trees into the yards. Johnny Peterson had a portable saw, and he cut the wood into blocks for us. We couldn't pay him, but thankfully he was happy to take wood for payment. He cut that up and sold it to the people in town, and probably made a pretty penny on it too. Henry and the boys took turns splitting the wood and piling it up on the north side of the house. We always had more than we needed.

That first winter, just after the first snow had fallen, I looked out the window and saw two Indians, natives I guess they call them now. Anyway, they were walking toward the house and I was terrified. I ran outside to the back of the house yelling for Henry to come.

"They are going to scalp us, I know they are," I sobbed.

He swore and walked with me back to the front

door. When he saw who was coming he laughed and went out to greet them. A few minutes later he came back and said, "have you got any fresh butter, they want to trade."

I was still sobbing because I was so scared. "Yes by the spring. They can have it all if they promise not to hurt us," I replied.

The two men waited patiently outside while he went back to the spring. I stood at the door watching. When he returned he gave them three pounds of butter and, in return, they gave Henry some fresh fish. They were all laughing at something and I had a feeling it was me.

After they left I asked Henry "what was so funny?"

"They wanted to know how I could live with a woman who screeched so loud. He told them he was used to it and didn't hear the noise any more. To me he said. "Sarah, these people are our neighbors, they won't hurt you. In fact we can learn a lot from them.

Then he got that devilish look in his eye, "If you aren't careful they will give you the Indian name of woman who screeches a lot and you don't want to be known as that do you?"

As usual Henry was right.

You know something Elyse. When we lived on the prairies I complained about how overworked I was, but that was nothing to getting started here. The biggest thing was that I was lonely. I was used to seeing friends and family nearly every day. We rarely saw any of Henry's family because they were working just as hard as we were. I wrote long letters home but it wasn't the same thing.

The boys weren't very old when Henry taught them to hunt. Ivan was a good shot and often he would go out and bring back a chicken or a rabbit for supper. When we were out of fresh meat, he and Henry would shoot a moose or a deer.

One of the neighbor ladies taught me how to can moose meat. I had a few empty jars left and Henry picked me up a dozen more in town. I filled them with meat, added salt and pepper and the boiled them in the canner for three hours. Sure was good for stew in the winter or when there was unexpected company for supper.

The next spring Henry and the boys dug me a root cellar for the preserves, potatoes and carrots we wanted to keep over the winter. That first year was a real learning process for me. Sometimes I went berry picking with the neighbors and made jam and jelly which went in there too. Life on the homestead was definitely harder than living on the prairies.

That first Christmas I unravelled two of my old sweaters and knit the boys new socks and mitts. Henry splurged and bought some oranges and candy for Christmas morning. The only time I left the farm that winter was to go to mass at one of the neighbor's homes.

I was expecting, and in February Baby Helen was born. Henry made her a beautiful crib of pine wood, and she slept beside our bed. She was a beautiful baby with deep blue eyes, and lots of black curly hair. The only time she cried was when she was hungry. When she was awake, she just lay in her bed and looked around. I was over joyed to finally have a baby girl.

That April the boys got the whooping cough, and the nearest doctor and hospital were twelve miles away. In those days you had to pay fifteen dollars a year to be able to use the hospital, and then another dollar fifty a day if you went there. We didn't have any money for a doctor or the hospital.

I did everything I could; I spoon fed those boys tea and honey to stop their coughing. I burned sulphur on the stove to kill the germs, and used cold water from the spring to bring down their fevers.

They were getting better then Baby Helen got sick. She was so small, and coughed until she threw up. Every cough ended in a whoop. After that, she would be too tired to nurse. For five days and nights I fed her tea and honey from a spoon, and walked the floor with her. I pleaded with God to help her get better. But, in the end, her little body just gave out and she stopped breathing. I was holding her in my arms when she gave a little sigh and then she was gone. We buried her up the road at the Cross Roads cemetery. There were lots of babies buried that spring.

I cried for days and I wanted to die too. I thought I was going to go crazy with grief. My breasts were sore, full of milk, and there was no baby to feed on them. It was all I could do to put the meals on the table. Now, I could understand how my mother felt watching her son slip into the sea.

Finally, one day Henry came to me "Sarah, you have to put this behind you. Pull yourself together. There is work to be done. The boys and I can't do this alone. We need you!"

Somehow we managed to get through this terrible time, but a piece of my heart is buried with my little girl. After a while living got easier. Sometimes I picked wild flowers and walked up to the cemetery to lay them on her little grave. Often I sat there and cried. If Henry knew, he never said anything to me. I have a feeling Henry used to do visit her too. We simply didn't talk about it. Twelve months later, little Anna was born."

* * *

Coming from some vague place I can hear someone calling my name.

"Mom, mom can you hear me? We are all here with you and plan on staying. We love you!"

I tried to say something, but no sound came out. I tried to move my hand to let them know I could hear them, but nothing happened. "Don't cry my children. I am still here for you."

"Do you think she can hear us?" a voice asked. "I heard someone say once that the hearing is the last thing to go on a person. I am sure she knows we are here. It's important that we keep talking to her."

Slowly I drifted back to my memories. Where did the years of my life go? They went by so fast.
I wish I could remember more.

Twelve

I must have dozed off. The sounds of voices wake me up but I am having a hard time making sense of what they are saying.

"How long do you think she will stay like this? Do you think she will ever wake up again Doctor?"

"I can't say for sure. She is a very determined lady, but her heart isn't strong any more. We will keep her comfortable and hydrated for now; any changes will likely come in the next twenty four hours."

"Do you think she is in pain?"

"I don't think so. She isn't acting like she is. I think she is tired and resting. Time will tell us what we want to know. You must remember she is ninety years old. There is only so much medication and determination can do. Her body is tired and deserving of rest. I think you need to prepare yourselves and your families for the worst, and hope for the best."

"Don't worry mom, you're not alone. We are taking turns; one of us is with you all the time." I feel Ruth squeeze my hand.

Henry and the children were my life. I wonder if they know how much they mean to me. After losing Helen each one of them was like a precious gift from above.

* * *

Elyse had a sparkling personality that drew people to her She smiled often and laughed freely. She didn't walk; she seemed to bounce in and bounce out. Sarah was amazed at the energy she had. *What I wouldn't give to have her energy bottled and be able to drink from it every day.*

When Elyse came the next morning she was very quiet. She had a sheaf of papers clipped together and a small white photo album in her hand.

"Is something wrong Elyse, you seem to be very quiet today. Is Rachel still giving you a hard time? Do I need to speak to her again?"

"There is nothing wrong gram. I haven't heard from her since she came to my room." she replied, but Sarah didn't believe her.

"Here," she said handing Sarah the papers. "This is what I have written so far, I would like you to go over it and make sure I didn't make any mistakes. I also added some of the stories I have heard around town about you and Henry."

"I hope they were good ones." Sarah teased.

Elyse laughed. "I guess you have to read them to find out."

Sarah didn't reach out and take them right away. "I trust you Elyse. My eyes are not what they used to be. What else have you got there?"

Her eyes glistened with tears. "Mom e-mailed these to me and I made an album for you."

"What is it child?"

Elyse handed the small album to Sarah. "These are copies of the pictures grandfather had from when he was younger. I thought you might like to see them."

"You miss him very much don't you Elyse?" Sarah asked gently. She was aware of the hurt and pain on Elyse's face.

"Wiping tears from her eyes Elyse replied, "Yes very much. I can't imagine going home and not seeing him there. I wish I could tell him about you and his brothers and sisters, He missed so much by not coming home. He might have not been so lonely."

"Elyse, don't so that to yourself. Ivan made his decisions a long time ago. We can't change what happened. It's like my Henry used to say "what's done is done.""

Sometimes I can't help thinking about the "what if's." What if I had refused to let Ivan go with the threshing crew? What if I had known he was in the

Navy, not the army, would we have been able to find him? The thing is Elyse; we have no way of changing the past."

Elyse sat quietly for a while, and then she smiled. "Come to think about it, if Grandpa had done anything different I wouldn't have been born."

Sarah laughed, "at least we know he did something right.

Elyse started to giggle. "Maybe you should tell that to Rachel."

"Enough of that. We have talked enough about me and Henry, how about you tell me more about your grandfather. Maybe it will help you understand how and why he left but first you need to understand life was quite different back then. There were few ways of communication."

Elise smiled at the old lady. "He was no angel gram."

"I believe that. Why would he be any different than the other boys? They had too much of their father in them. Tell me more about him. What kind of man was he?"

"I'm not sure what to say. To me he was the best grandfather a girl could ask for, although there are some who may not agree.

Grandma Iris told me that at one time he had a bad drinking problem and was always getting into fights. She used to say, "Once he married me he began to smarten up. He knew that I wasn't about to put up with his nonsense."

"Grandpa drove himself hard, never quitting until the job was done. Anybody who ever worked for him used to say he was demanding to work for, but fair. He could fix anything, especially cars and tractors. One time, I went crying to him because my brothers had pulled my doll's head off. He fixed it better than new, and then told the boys to leave me alone. If they didn't, they would have to deal with him."

"Did it help?"

"For a few days."

Sarah chuckled. *So like a child to remember the small things.* She could picture Elyse running after her brothers trying to get her doll back.

"He had secrets Gram. We heard that many years ago he had been in jail for beating someone up, but when we asked he wouldn't admit it was true.

He was married before he met Grandma Iris, but that's all we know. He told grandma he had been married before but when we tried to find out more, she wouldn't say a word.

Sometimes when he came to the house he was louder than normal. I was afraid of him when he was like that. Mom told me that was usually when he had been drinking. She knew I was scared and would tell me to go play in my room. I know he would have never hurt me bit I didn't feel safe. When I was older I got over that fear but still didn't like to be around him when he had been drinking."

"By what you have told me so far he sounds a lot like Henry. He always seemed to be shouting, but that's just the way he was."

"After he married Grandma Iris he bought the farm. At first it was only one quarter of land but he was shrewd business man and built it up to ten quarters. He had cattle, raised horses and sold many of his bulls to the rodeo owners who lived nearby.

In his early days he drank hard, worked hard and played hard. He told us stories of where he had been and some of the things he had done. By the sound of it, some of the things he did would have made you hair curl."

"You said there were three boys?"

"Yes, my dad Bobby, Uncle Joe, and Uncle Billy - Uncle Joe has three boys and Uncle Billy has four. Dad was the youngest. I have two older brothers, Tim and Randy. Like I told you before I am the youngest and only girl of the bunch.

I clearly remember the time I wanted a Princess Barbie doll. All of my friends had one, but dad couldn't afford to buy one for me. One evening grandpa Ivan arrived at the house slightly tipsy, with two of the most beautiful and expensive Barbie dolls I have ever seen. He had a real soft spot when it came to kids, and especially me."

. "All the boys were like that. Full of pee and vinegar but could be counted on when they were needed the most." Sarah said.

"Grandpa helped the boys build houses on the farm when they got married, but not all in the same yard. He used to say "there is nothing more important than family." When he retired from farming him and grandma stayed on the home quarter and each of the boys were given three quarters.

Grandma Iris died five years ago and after that he seemed really lost. I think he was lonely after she passed. He would help the boys in the spring and fall with the farming and the cattle. He had a workshop where he built things and puttered away fixing old cars. He used to take them different places to show them off.

"I wonder why he never came back home," Sarah said sadly.

"I don't know the answer to that Gram and now that I think about it, I don't know if he could answer that himself. I think he always meant to, but kept putting it off. Maybe after a long time he though you wouldn't want to see him."

With a gentle smile Sarah asked, "Are you still mad at us Elyse? Are you sorry you came?"

"No, I only wish I had found you sooner. You

would have been proud of him Gram. He was kind and would give you the shirt off his back if you needed it. Like I said, there were things he never talked about so we never knew for sure how he felt. On other things he made sure we knew exactly where he was coming from. Sighing wistfully she added, "I think he would be pleased to know I came here.

Ivan. Sarah had put him out of my mind until Elise showed up. *Thank you Lord for bringing her to us*.

"Now it's my turn.to tell you more about him," Sarah said, settling back in her chair. "Your grandpa was a real character even when he was younger. Even as a kid if a person asked him for help, he did what he could. If you wanted to fight, he was prepared to do that too. Most of the time, he came out on the winning side.

Your grandfather was a big baby when he was born, nearly nine pounds. Henry was ecstatic that his first born was a son. Somehow it didn't seem fair, I did all the work and he got all of the glory. We named him after Henry's grandfather. I swore after that I was never having any more children, but we both know how that went.

Right from the start he was hungry and curious, seemed like I could never get that boy filled up. From the time he could walk he was Henry's shadow, and followed him around everywhere. If I couldn't find Ivan, all I had to do was find Henry and the two of them would be together.

He had a sharp mind and tried to copy whatever Henry did. He was two when I caught him trying to take Henry's shotgun apart to clean it. The two of them would often go hunting together and by the time he was five, he was shooting gophers and bringing home the odd rabbit and partridge for supper.

We did our best to send him to school, but he hated it. I fought with him every day to get him out the door. We tried to force him, but when we moved north that was the end of his schooling. All he ever had was a grade three education, but that never stopped him.

He and Henry worked side by side, clearing trees, ploughing the land and planting the crops. Even as a child he showed a talent for fixing things and the neighbours were always bringing him something to work on.

When he was fourteen Minnie Hines brought in a threshing crew from the south to take off her crop. They were looking for help so him and Henry signed on. The pay was a dollar a day and we needed the money.

When they were done at Minnie's, the foreman asked Ivan to keep working with them because they had a couple more places to do in the area. I can still see Ivan and Henry walking around the yard discussing whether he should go or not.

When he came inside Henry said me, "Sarah, I told the boy he could stay working with the threshing crew until they leave the area."

"No, he is too young" I protested. "We need him here. Who is going to help you get your crop off?"

"I said he could go Sarah. Leave him be. The other boys are big enough to start doing more."

"When the foreman came to pick him up the next morning I cried. I wasn't ready to see my children start to leave home. I didn't talk to Henry for the rest of the day.

While the crew was close to home he would show up long enough to get his clothes washed and leave us some money. Eventually, with Henry's blessing, not mine, Ivan left with the crew, and that was the last time I saw him. At first there were several notes a month each with a few dollars. We knew he was working in Minnesota when the letters stopped coming regularly,

When the war started he wrote and said he was joining the American Army as a Seabee. I worried about him all the time, afraid he was going to get himself shot or killed. Every night I prayed for his safety.

On Mother's day, in 1942 I got a card that said he

was helping build a road and an air base in Alaska. He had asked for a transfer to the Pacific but wasn't sure when it would be coming through. Later on we heard that there had been a battle with the Japanese on one of the islands.

I didn't know if he was still there or if he had got his transfer. We never heard from him again. I stayed mad at Henry until the day he died for letting Ivan leave with that threshing crew.

I knew in my heart he wasn't dead. A mother knows those things. Henry never forgave himself either for letting the boy go. After a while we simply accepted the fact that he wasn't coming back and had probably been killed. I prayed one day we would find out the truth.

By now besides Ivan, Joshua, Jacob, Mathew and Baby Anna had been born. Life was hard and the kids and the farm work kept me busy from sun up to sun down. When I look back now I don't know how I did all I had to. We were happy."

Suddenly something Elyse said struck me. "Elyse, when you first arrived, you said your grandfather was in the Navy?"

'Yes, the Seabees were part of the navy." Elyse stated in a matter of fact voice. "Everybody knows that."

Sarah felt her heart begin to pound. "Oh my goodness, we thought Ivan was in the Army, No wonder we couldn't find him. We were looking in the wrong place all the time.

Now it begins to make more sense. We didn't have much to go on, just where he was, and then nothing. Knowing this now explains a lot of things. Still, there was really no excuse. He knew where we lived, and our address. He could have just as easily contacted us. I am just happy to know that he survived that awful fighting. I guess, after a while, he realized we were getting old and had probably passed on. He never did know about the other brothers and sisters he had."

After Elyse left I asked myself *could this whole mess have been avoided if we had known he was in the Navy not the Army. Would we have been able to find him? Nobody will ever know the answer to that question. I am so glad that she found us and I finally know the truth.*

Thirteen

We stayed on the homestead until Minnie Hines put her land up for sale. Two quarters of land, a house and a brand new barn for ten thousand dollars. Henry went over and talked with Minnie. She agreed to sell to us and for the next three years we would pay her each fall when the crop came off

I was worried sick. "How are we going to pay for this Henry?" I asked him one day.

"Don't you worry Sarah? The Lord will provide as he always does." He never worried about things like that. When he made up his mind about something, he just went ahead and did it – didn't do me much good to argue with him.

From that time on, every time I shipped eggs and cream, and every dollar Ivan sent us I put away - a kind of an emergency fund you call it today. I didn't tell Henry because he would have been embarrassed to ask for the money if he needed it.

The next spring, after Ivan left, we moved to the Hines place. Everything we had in that small house fit into two wagons. The new house had three bedrooms, a cellar and a full loft upstairs. The boys had one bedroom, the girls the other, and Henry and

I had one. The well was outside. We didn't have the power yet. Minnie had paid for it before she decided to sell but it was another year before it was put in.

I was sorry to leave our old place. The first chance I had, I went back and dug up some of my roses, perennials and rhubarb plants. I couldn't see them go to waste. The best part about moving was that I didn't feel so isolated. We were on the main road to town and people were always stopping by.

That spring Henry seeded the land on both places. The rent on the homestead was paid until fall. He put in oats, barley and wheat and, at the Hines place built a new pen for the pigs with a rail fence. Fat lot of good that did, they still got out. We moved our two sheep into the north pasture with the cows.

Life got a little easier once we moved to the Hines place. The first fall we had a bumper crop. The granaries were filled with wheat, oats and barley. Henry sold most of the wheat and sent the money to Minnie. Naturally that left us with little, so Henry decided he would make extra money making moonshine and selling it to the neighbours and at parties and dances.

After we moved., I got into town a little more often because I sometimes went in with a neighbor, and I joined the Ladies Aide group, which met once a month. Occasionally I needed to get away from the kids and have some adult company.

Henry loved to play whist, so we were invited to quite a few card parties or we held them at our place. I wasn't very good. Usually he would get upset with me because I played the wrong card. I don't know how many times I told him "Henry it's only a card game," but he liked to win.

By now we had an old Ford truck. Henry made a deal with Ralph Granger at the store. Ralph gave him fuel, and Henry paid him in moonshine. Ralph then sold the moonshine out the back door. Ralph was an honest man. If he got more for the moonshine than Henry owed for his gas they split the difference in cash. That way they both made money.

Rachel was too little, so the boys helped their dad. Everybody said that he made a nice smooth brew, the best in the country. The older boys would go to dances and take some to sell, though sometimes I think they drank more than they sold.

I used to say to him, "Henry one of these days you are going to get caught."

Each time he would say the same thing back to me "Sarah, don't you worry about this. Me and the boys are careful, and Ralph will never tell."

I think he finally realized what I was talking about the day when he almost did get caught. Up until then I think he thought what he was doing was a game.

He and Joe Miller were going to town with the

team and wagon to ship some pigs and make a delivery to Ralph. A person never knew what was going to happen when those two got together. Anyway, they were about five miles from the farm when they saw a car coming and someone waving a handkerchief out the side window. When the car came around the speed curve, they realized it was a police car.

Henry knew that if they stopped him and found his moonshine, he would be in big trouble. He turned the wagon around, and Joe climbed into the back and pushed the pigs out onto the road. Pigs aren't that smart and will only move when they want to. The police had to stop and push every one of those ornery pigs off the road into the ditch.

Ralph told us later the police came to his store and demanded he take them to Henry's farm. They suspected the two of them were in cahoots with each other. Maybe they thought Ralph would incriminate Henry by saying something out of place. Ralph explained he couldn't refuse, because then they might suspect something.

Anyway, Henry and Joe hoped the pigs would slow the police car down enough, so they could get home first. The horses ran into the yard at full speed. Joe jumped off the wagon and ran into the house, while Henry and the team headed straight for the barn.

"Sarah," Joe hollered at me, "Henry said to get rid of all the moonshine you have in the house. The police are right behind us."

I had one small barrel in the porch, so I opened the cellar door and pushed it down the stairs. I heard the barrel break apart when it hit the bottom. I had no sooner closed the cellar door when the police car came into the yard.

Henry casually walked down from the barn, and met them out by the gate. The three of them, Henry, Ralph, and Joe, stood in the yard talking, while the police searched the house and yard. I wasn't any too happy about them walking over my nice clean floors with their dusty boots, and I told them so in no uncertain terms.

Of course they found the broken barrel downstairs. I even had to give them a clean jar so they could scoop up a sample of the dirt and take it with them to be analyzed. Later, we heard the sample was too contaminated to be of any good. Sargent Brady gave Henry a stern lecture about the consequences of selling moonshine and what could happen if he got caught, and then they left.

Actually it was quite funny because he was one of Ralph's best customers, and knew exactly what was going on. Somehow they all managed to keep a straight face through the whole affair, and it turned out that a new fellow on the force was trying to make a name for himself.

After everybody left I said to him, "Henry Walker, you get out of this moonshine business right now. You almost got caught, and it will take weeks for that raw liquor smell to get out of that cellar, if it ever does."

"Now, now Sarah" he replied, "They didn't catch me this time did they?" When he looked at me he had that silly grin on his face that showed up every time he got caught doing something he wasn't supposed to. I had a hard time staying mad at him. It took the two of them the rest of the day to round up the pigs and bring them home. They waited a couple of days before trying again."

Elyse was laughing. "I know grandfather would have been right in there if he had been around."

"There was one other time," Sarah continued "he just about got caught. He went to town to deliver four gallons of moonshine to Ralph. The jugs were sitting on the counter when two policemen came in the front door of the store. Good thing Ralph's counter was located near the back of the store.

Ralph grabbed two of the jugs, and put them on the floor behind the counter. Henry said to Ralph "I have to get about my business. Look after your customers. I can fill these two jugs with kerosene myself, and will leave the money in the back for you."

Nonchalantly he picked up the other two jugs, pretending they were empty, and walked to the back of the store. There he put the two jugs into an open cupboard; closed the doors, picked up two jugs of kerosene and walked out the back door. When the coast was clear, and the police were out of sight, Henry took Ralph's jugs of kerosene back to him.

They had quite a laugh over that one too. When I look back, I am truly amazed that neither Henry nor the boys ever got caught. Elyse, you have to understand one thing, Henry was careful and made just a few extra dollars for us to live on. That was enough. As much as I hate to admit it, sometimes that money made the difference between eating and going hungry.

After that, I made Henry move his still across the road. I was surprised that he agreed with me that it would be safer there. After that one visit from the police he was concerned about them showing up when he wasn't home. He didn't want me or the children put in that position again.

I used to let the pigs and chickens roam freely around the yard. It really didn't matter where they went, as long as they stayed out of my garden. I always had that part fenced off, but more than once I caught them in there.

Well, this one day I heard a funny noise and looked out the kitchen window in time to see one of the pigs fall over dead. Just like that. One second it was walking, the next it was flat on its back, all four feet up in the air.

I ran outside and saw four more dead pigs lying between the house and the pen. I heard a squawking sound, and my two best laying hens fell from the sky, right at my feet.

I didn't know what to do. Henry and the boys were working in the field and Rachel was the only one home with me. The two of us gathered up the dead chickens, and laid them in a row beside the hen house. The pigs were too heavy to move. I knew I should cut their throats and bleed them, but I didn't know if the meat would be any good. Besides, that was Henry's job. I had never done it before.

Then it hit me, and I felt sick to my stomach. If all my chickens and pigs were dead, I didn't know how we could replace them. Harvest was a long ways away and we didn't have any money to speak of, certainly not enough to buy more animals.

I was sitting at the kitchen table crying my eyes out when I heard Henry come up the road on the tractor, and then turn into the quarter across the road. He wasn't there very long before he drove into our yard. Rachel and I ran outside to tell him what had happened. He got off the tractor and knelt down beside the dead pig.

"Henry, they are all dead, every one of them.

There are dead pigs and chickens lying all over this yard. Do you think they could have got into some poison?"

"Yep, they did that all right. Wasn't poison, rot gut is more like it," he replied. "Somehow they got the door of the mash shed open, and ate most of what was there. They aren't dead, they are drunk. That batch was just about ready to run off. Not much left now," He said petulantly. "Stupid pigs. Go back inside, they will sleep it off."

Sure enough over the next few hours the pigs got up and staggered to their pens. Eventually, the chickens all made it into the hen house, though there weren't many eggs for the next few days. One thing I did notice was that they never crossed the road again."

"Is this a true story Gram," Elyse asked," or are you teasing me?" She was wiping tears from her eyes from laughing so hard.

"Every word is true Elyse. Your great-grandfather never did settle down, and his boys were pretty much the same way."

Fourteen

"Gram," Elyse asked one day, "something puzzles me. How did you manage to do everything you had to do each day? You had gardening, baking, three meals a day to cook, clothes to wash and mend, and I don't know what else to fit into your day and all of that without power or running water. I can't begin to imagine what your day was like. I used to ask grandfather, but all he ever talked about was getting the crop off and playing in the barn. It doesn't sound like you had very much help or had time to have fun."

"Yes child, I did work hard, but a person did what they had to do to get by. If I didn't, there wasn't anybody else to take over. Henry was impossible when it came to women's chores.

You are right though; there wasn't much time for fun. Now, when I look back, I don't know how I managed. I guess I did the same thing as my mother. She taught us girls everything she knew, and when my girls got older, I taught them to help me. From the time they were little they had chores to do every day. The boys helped Henry outside and the girls helped me in the house. Remind me to tell you some of the things we did for fun. It wasn't always work and no play.

One of the chores I enjoyed the most was working in my garden and I was always proud of it. My biggest problem was keeping the pigs and deer out of it. Each spring, I spent days planting the thing. I always put in lots of onion, potatoes, turnips, cabbage, carrots, things we could keep over the winter in the root cellar. If there wasn't much rain, I had a barrel on a wagon and watered each plant with a tin dipper. Every spare moment I had I used for picking weeds. In the spring the early dandelion greens were a real treat and we ate them as salad greens. My biggest worry was frost, either a late one in the spring or an early one in the fall. More than once my hard work came to nothing.

All summer and fall I picked rhubarb, raspberries, wild strawberries, high and low bush cranberries and saskatoons, and made hundreds of jars of jelly and jam. The jars that didn't set I used for syrup for pancakes.

. Henry built me some shelves for the cellar, and I stored the jars of canning down there. I'm sure each fall there were at least five hundred jars on the shelves. If we couldn't afford to buy more sugar, I dried the fruit and vegetables and stored them lard pails in the root cellar. These I used for pies or soups.

The first summer we were at the Hines place Henry built me a summer kitchen. It wasn't much, three walls, a roof, a large cook stove and a work bench. I did everything out there, or as much as I could. Traipsing back and forth was easier than heating the house when it was hot. No matter where I was there were always lots of flies. After a while I just got used to them. We used the summer kitchen for everything imaginable, and I don't know how I would have managed without it.

Minnie had planted two apple and crab apple trees and what I didn't use I gave to the neighbours. Each fall Henry bought a hundred pounds of sugar. When that ran out I usually couldn't get any more. He always made several batches of crab apple Brandy, which he only brought out for special occasions. He always gave the priest two bottle for medicinal purposes."

Elyse giggled, "Whatever you say Gram."

Sarah replied indignantly, "that's what he told us, but we all knew he enjoyed a nip or two in the evening."

"Where was I? I canned the peas and beans in jars. I would wash, shell or cut the vegetables, put them in jars with water and salt and then cook them in my tin boiler on top of the stove. The beans took about three hours for each batch, and I could only do nine jars at a time.

Henry, and I and the kids would usually spend one whole day shredding cabbage with the kraut cutter for sauerkraut. We usually made three forty five gallon barrels. We would fill them up with cabbage, sprinkle the layers with salt, tamp it down until the juice appeared, and then add some more. When it got close to being full I put whole heads in so I had sour cabbage for cabbage rolls. After that, we put the wooden top back on the barrel and then some big rocks for weight.

This was a smelly process. We kept it outside while it was fermenting because it stunk to high heaven. In the winter I used a hatchet to hack of chunks off for supper. Everything else was put into the root cellar and was packed between layers of sawdust and ice. . Nothing got wasted on the farm, there always a use for it."

"Gram, you make me tired just listening to you."

"You young ones have it easy. If you want something you go to the store and buy it. We weren't able to do that. Unless Henry took odd jobs, we were always short of money in the winter. What little we did have, we saved for spring seeding. To tell you the truth it wasn't a big deal back then. All of our neighbors were in the same situation, and we figured out ways to make do.

Each fall we butchered a cow and two pigs, and kept the meat in the ice house. I rendered the fat for lard in the oven and used it for cooking and baking. The boys waited anxiously for the cracklings. That was the rinds of the pieces after all of the fat had been cooked out. If I remember correctly they tasted better than candy. The heart and liver were the special treat that we cooked and ate for supper on butchering day. Henry used to tell people I used everything except the squeal on a pig. Often, we would go help the neighbors on butchering day and then they would come help us.

Chicken was our only fresh meat and we usually had that for Sunday supper. In the morning I would send Henry out to butcher the chicken, and then pluck the feathers and soak it in salt water until I was ready to cook. When the boys shot geese or ducks, I kept the down for quilts and used the feathers for pillows.

Usually one or two of the boys shot a moose in the fall. I canned many jars of moose meat for stew. Henry would save one of the smaller pigs until then, kill it, grind up the meat and add this to ground moose meat for sausage. He smoked the sausage, and we stored it in the root cellar with the other meat. We often traded the Indians meat for fish. We always raised one or two turkeys and at Christmas Henry had the honour of killing one for dinner.

Lord I hated those turkeys. They were mean and chased whoever came close to them. I still remember the time I sent Rachel to gather the eggs, and the next thing I heard was her swearing a blue streak out. I looked out the door to see what was wrong. One of those pesky turkeys was chasing her and she was throwing my fresh eggs at it, trying to make it leave her alone.

Keeping those boys filled up was something else. They were big strapping men and always hungry. I made eight loaves of bread three times a week. On top of this were cakes, pies, cookies and biscuits. At butchering and harvesting time the neighbours helped each other and there were plenty of extra mouths to feed."

Elyse was mesmerized, listening to Sarah tell her story. She shook her head. "I'm glad we don't have to work that hard today Gram, I don't know if any of us could."

"Probably not," Sarah chuckled. "I doubt if I could again, but that was what was necessary. We didn't have the modern conveniences you do today.

In the fall, after the harvest was done and money was more plentiful, Henry and I would go to town and buy most of the supplies we needed for the winter - coffee, tea, sugar, flour, baking powder, oatmeal, molasses, rice, beans and so on. We never went hungry, though sometimes the cupboard seemed bare. I learned to make do with what we had and be very creative.

I didn't like going to town much when the war was on. Some of the town's people didn't take too kindly to us being German. There are always people in this world who are mean and nasty and can't mind their own business. They would call us "krauts, Nazis" and accuse us of spying. I usually did my best to ignore them, finish what I came to do, and then go home.

It was harder for Henry though. The name calling used to make him mad. I think the reason was because he had two boys in the service overseas fighting, and the fact that he was born in the United States.

I'll never forget that one time when he went to town. He parked the team of horse at Jim Taylor's livery barn. Jim always kept a bottle to share with his friends and, of course, they had a couple of drinks. Henry decided he better do what he came for, or else he might get carried away and forget. When he was finished, he went back to Jim's and they decided to finish the bottle before Henry left for home. He told me apparently it was half empty so they decided it would be a shame to leave it that way.

Around supper time Henry finally decided to leave for home. When he went to get into the wagon two young men standing on the sidewalk began calling him names. They shouted at him, "Go back home Kraut. Go back to Germany where you belong."

Well my Henry took offence to this, and the fight was on. It didn't take him much to get riled up when he was drinking. When the horse and wagon pulled into the yard it was dark already, and I admit, I was starting to get a little worried.

Henry was a sight to behold. His face was cut up and bloody, knuckles scraped and swollen, his shirt was torn, and he stunk of liquor and sweat. If he looked that bad, I hated to see what the other guy looked like.

The boys and I managed to get him into the house, which was no easy feat. "Sarah," he said "you should see the other guys" then he passed out on the floor. Good thing those horses knew how to find their way back home.

I sent the boys out to bring in the supplies, feed the horses and put them into the barn. We left the wagon in the yard. I was so mad at Henry that I left him lying on the floor until he woke up the next morning. Later I asked Jim Taylor why he hadn't help Henry out. Two against one wasn't fair.

"Mrs. Walker," he replied, "Henry was drunk enough and ornery enough that he was doing fine all by himself. Those boys didn't stand a chance. When the boys limped off, Henry got into his wagon and drove off, never even said good bye. After that thrashing, I don't think them Culver twins did anymore name calling. What made it worse for them is that their pa made them apologize the next time Henry came to town."

Fifteen

Glancing at Elyse, with her eyes twinkling Sarah said "the three things I appreciated the most throughout the years was electricity, running water and indoor plumbing. Many people are surprised when I say this, but they have no idea what it was like before.

A person hasn't lived until they have used an outdoor biffy with a hornets nest in a corner. A person did his business and got out as fast as he could, and hopefully without getting stung in the process. Henry did his best to knock the nests down but within two or three days they were back.

Once a week everybody got a bath, whether they needed it or not. I heated the water on the stove, and then filled the galvanized wash tub. The youngest would go first, and then I worked my way up. If the water got cold, I added more from the kettle. When they were finished I emptied the tub and heated fresh water for myself. You have no idea how I longed to be able to sit and soak, but that was not the case.

At the homestead we packed water from the spring by the bucketful. The black cook stove had a reservoir on one side which I kept filled. The fire from the coal and wood stove kept the water warm. We had a barrel by the stove, and each morning one of the boys would fill it then I filled the reservoir as needed throughout the day.

We used water from the creek for the animals, chickens and the garden. The spring never completely froze, so in the winter we moved the water barrel from the wagon to the sleigh so we could water the animals. When we moved to the Hines house the well was closer to the house which made living easier for me.

Monday was always wash day. The day before I would fill one of the extra barrels with water and add ashes from the stove to make the water softer, and the clothes come out cleaner. Early in the morning I set out my wash tubs, filling one with hot water and the other with cold for rinsing. I had a metal plunger, looked like one of those toilet plungers we have today, which I used to wash the jeans and coveralls. I scrubbed the more delicate and white things with soap on the scrub board. I braced the wooden frame against my tummy and scrubbed the clothes up and down on the glass ridges. It was awkward when I was pregnant, and bothered my back.

When I see people changing clothes two or three times a day now I shudder. Back then the boys wore their clothes for a week except for socks and underwear. I made them put clean ones on every day. We kept our best for church and took them off as soon as we got home.

I made my own soap and the lye made my hands sore. I wrung the clothes by hand then put them into the rinse water to soak. Then I would wring them out again and hang them on the clothesline. I'm sure that's why I have such bad arthritis in my hands today. When the kids were small, Henry helped by keeping the tubs full of clean water. We usually emptied them two or three times before I was finished. When the boys got older, they would help. In the summer, I used the summer kitchen to heat the water. Of course, in the winter I was inside.

Mother taught me to wash the whites first, then lights, and then go by degree of dirtiness. I still did that until I moved in here. Winter and summer I hung everything outside. I had a clothesline behind the stove and would move the frozen clothes inside to finish drying. Usually by the time everything was dry, it was time to start over again.

One day Henry brought home a gas powered washing machine. In the winter the fumes stunk up the place, but the smell was worth it. There was an agitator inside and when the motor started it would turn. It sure beat standing over a scrub board. We still had to pack and empty the water, and I still had to wring the clothes by hand. On wash days my back would get so sore I could barely walk, and my wrists and hands would ache for days. In the spring I made Henry move that smelly washer outside so we wouldn't have to choke on the fumes.

After we got the power, I got an electric washer with a wringer on the top. No more wringing clothes out by hand or dipping the dirty water out. I still had to pack and heat the water, and then empty the dirty water out, but there was a pump so that part was much easier. When the girls got older I'd have them take turns staying home from school to help me. The job was betting to be too much for one person."

Elyse was content to sit back and let Sarah talk. She loved hearing the stories and the more Sarah talked the more animated she became. Her hands would move through the air, her face would light up and she laughed often. Elyse caught glimpses of the no nonsense, easy going person she must have been when she was younger.

"My mother taught me to keep a clean house. No matter how hard I scrubbed, the walls of the Hines house seemed dirty all the time One day I decided I to plaster them. Henry thought I was crazy, but went along with my idea anyway. Not that he had much choice in the matter.

I talked him into mixing a pile of dirt with no rocks with clean oat straw. The kids tamped the mixture with their bare feet and Henry kept adding water until it was the right consistency. When it was ready, the kids brought the mixture inside to me then I troweled it onto the walls. Before the plaster was completely dry I smoothed it out by using my trowel and clean water. Every few hours I went over it with a cloth and water to make sure it dried slowly and didn't crack. When the plaster was completely dry I white washed it. It took us most of the summer to get the kitchen and living room done, but what a difference.

I brought an old treadle Singer sewing machine when

we moved north, and saved sugar and flour sacks to make curtains. The Saskatoon berries were in season so I boiled them, kept the berries for pies, and then used the juice to dye the material. I must say the rooms looked pretty good when I was finished.

That winter Henry and I glued gunny sacks to the wall in the kitchen beginning about three feet from the bottom. First I unravelled the thread, and then he would paste the open bags on the wall. When we were finished we put several coats of varnish on top. This stopped the boys from putting holes in the wall when they leaned back on their chairs.

Each month I took the old straw out of the mattresses and put in clean wheat straw. I was always worried about getting bedbugs in my house. Once they got in, it was near impossible to get rid of them."

"I can't imagine having to do that. I guess kids my age don't understand how good we have it," Elyse remarked

"You can say that again," Sarah replied. "Now when I look back, I was busy cooking, cleaning, sewing, knitting, washing or having babies. I made most of our clothing on that old sewing machine, especially the girl's dresses and the boy's shirts. Ralph always kept a good supply of yard goods in the store. The only thing was that many of us ended up looking alike.

When I was on the farm I wore pants, but always wore a dress into town or on Sunday.

Those boys were forever getting a hole in the knees of their pants, or losing a mitt, or wearing holes in their sock. I did the mending in the evenings but it was a thankless job. The next week there was just as much, and you can only mend some things so many times.

With most of Henry's family living around us ours became the meeting house. There was always someone coming or going. When we lived on the homestead we often went for weeks without seeing each other.

Since our house was the biggest, our family and neighbors gathered there for supper on Christmas day. The girls decorated the ceilings and windows with streamers, and made most of our decorations using a salt and flour mixture and my cookie cutters. After they were dry they either coloured or painted them and hung them on the tree. We made paper chains from newspaper and old catalogues to drape all around the branches.

Sometimes the priest came to say mass; other times we held our own service. Everyone brought food, and once we were done eating the cards came out. We always invited several of the local bachelors to join us so they wouldn't be alone.

We had ham, turkey, potatoes, turnips, carrots, buns, pickles, pie, plus some of the good old traditional German dishes. For the life of me I can't remember their names right now."

"That's okay Gram, maybe the names will come to

you later."

Every year we put on a Christmas concert at the school. Old Charlie Webber would be Santa Claus and hand out candy bags to the children. Each of the families put in a dollar to help pay for them. After the concert we had a social evening which usually ended with us standing around the piano singing carols. We would go home in the sleigh pulled by the horses. There was something about breathing in the cold crisp air and seeing stars in the sky that made this a special time.

In the later years, after the hall was built, we held a dance on New Year's Eve. Everybody went. The women usually stayed inside the hall, but the men often disappeared outside to have a drink. Of course, the women pretended not to know what they were doing. When the kids got tired we used our coats to make them a bed on the stage and let them sleep there.

In the old days, when we didn't have much money, the presents were new socks and mitts. I sewed rag dolls for the girls and little clothes for the dolls. Uncle Charlie was good with his hands and he made wooden cars and trucks for the boys. On Christmas Eve we gathered in the living room, and Henry would tell the children the story about Baby Jesus.

Things were different then. Now people rush around buying expensive presents. Even after we moved to town Christmas night and Boxing Day the house was filled with friends and family. Those were the good old days!"

"Did you go to church in town Gram?"

"No not until the later years. Once a month the priest came to our house to say mass and the neighbors would come. In the winter, if it was cold, he usually stayed over so he could travel home in the daylight. In the summer he always managed to find a way to stay for supper before leaving. If there were any baptism or confirmations he did those when he came for mass.

In the summer I taught catechism classes to the local and town kids so the older ones could have their first communion. For two weeks there were always ten or twelve extra kids to take care of. It was a lot of extra work but I never minded.

When we had a better car we started going to church in town on Sunday. As they got older the boys quit going to church except for weddings or funerals. I wanted them to bring their families up in the church, some did, and some didn't. Not much I can do about that now.

Once we moved into town, Henry had the phone put in. He didn't see any sense having one on the farm. He used to say "can't sit around waiting for the darn thing to ring." When coloured TV came to our area the boys all chipped in and bought us one for Christmas. Every time Henry would sit down to watch the darn thing he fell asleep. I liked to watch my stories in the afternoon.

It feels like life was much simpler then. Sometimes, I miss hearing the birds sing, watching the sun go down, listening to the silence or the wind whispering in the trees, but the thing I miss most is living on the farm.

Sixteen

Elyse settled quickly into the small town and into a daily routine. This town was different than those back home. The people were friendly, more laid back and the pace was much slower than she was used to. When the motel owner realized she was part of the Walker family he gave her a reduced rate. Before too long she was on first name basis with many of the local people.

Many of the older people she met had already heard of her and her connection to the Walker family. They were willing to share their stories and some remembered her grandfather as a boy. She added these anecdotes to her writing. Some Sarah disputed others she laughed and shook her head. "I had forgotten about that," she would say.

Elyse felt as if time was passing too fast, and that within a few days she would be leaving for home. *All good things must end but it is going to be hard to leave here.*

In the meantime Sarah had caught a cold and wasn't feeling well. She coughed so hard the spells wore her out. Elyse was becoming quite concerned about her. *She seems to be getting smaller every day.*

One morning she said to Sarah," this is too much

for you. I appreciate the stories and the time we have spent together, but you are not well. Taking care of yourself is more important than getting all of this history down, besides I have to leave in a few days."

"Elyse, I am not long for this world. I am ready to meet my maker and be with Henry again. I still have so much more I want to tell you and talking isn't hard work, I'm not finished yet."

Elyse got off her chair and kneeled in front of Sarah. Taking her by the hand she said "Gram this time has meant more to me than you will ever know. I know that when I leave I will probably never see you again, and that breaks my heart. My one wish is that grandfather had been in your life and you were part of ours all this time. I love you Gram. Thank you for accepting me as part of your family. I will always remember you and this special time we had together."

"I love you too Elyse. I can rest easily now knowing that Ivan had a good life and that you came to tell me about him. She winked at Elyse, "Now I want to tell you about my Henry."

Elyse smiled. "Okay Gram, if you insist. What about Grandpa Henry? How did the two of you survive all of those hard times? It sounds like he wasn't much of a talker."

"My Henry was a very handsome man. At least that's what I thought the first time I saw him, standing at the back of the church. He was tall, muscular and had those deep blue eyes that seemed to look right through you. His nose always appeared to be a little too large for his face, but it added character. I remember thinking how big his hands were. His deep loud voice always made him sound like he was hollering but actually he was a teddy bear underneath that hard shell. I guess growing up in a family of noisy boys one had to holler to be heard. That was just his way, but sometimes it put people off.

Those Walker boys were always in some sort of trouble. Mostly it was silly pranks, nothing too serious. Their dad, when he was still alive, made and sold moonshine so I guess that's who Henry learned his craft from.

He was always good to me. Sometimes he got too loud, and drank too much on Saturday night, but no matter what, he went to church every Sunday. Although we had many arguments, he never laid a hand on me. He was a deeply religious man, which I guess he learned from his mama.

He worked hard, often from sun up to sun down. Many a time he came into the house for supper and his hands were bleeding from cutting wood or digging out stumps in the field, It hurt him deeply when times got rough in Alton, and he couldn't find enough work to feed us. He flatly refused to take the dole from the government, as so many of our neighbours did. He didn't want to feel obligated to anybody.

He was a very stubborn man. Once he had his mind made up about something, he very rarely changed it and he always had a hard time admitting if he was wrong. He used to say to me "Sarah, you look after the house. My job is to keep you and the children warm and fed."

People thought he didn't have any feelings, but that wasn't true. He just didn't want others to see them. Sometimes what he said hurt me, like when Helen died, but as much as I hate to admit it he was usually right. He never meant to be cruel; he just came across sounding that way.

Henry had an uncanny way of figuring people out the first time he met them. He seemed to know right away who was honest and who wasn't. He knew who he could trust the first time he met them. There again, he was often right.

Granny Hubert, an older widow woman, lived five miles north of us, and we used to see her quite often. Henry always picked up her mail in town and she would always have a cup of tea ready when we took it to her. Often, I took her eggs and butter.

One day Granny Hubert's niece and her family arrived out of the blue. Granny took them in, no questions asked.

We met them the first time we went there and they seemed like nice people. After that when we went to see Granny her niece would stop us at the door with some sort of excuse. She was sleeping, or not feeling well, or something like that.

One day Henry said to me "that woman is pure evil and a liar. I don't like her and I don't trust her."

After the third time she wouldn't let Henry into the house, he went to the police. He asked around town, but nobody had seen Granny Hubert for weeks. The police started looking into things, and it turned out all of her family was in England. Allan Peters, the police officer, decided to go check on her and see for himself who these people were.

It was a good thing Allan decided to go when he did, or she would have died. What had gone on in that house was awful. The niece and her family were gone, and so were Granny's furniture, her old truck, and all of money she kept in the house. Most of us kept our money at home rather than put it into the bank, it was easier that way. Granny never told us how much they got away with.

Allan found her chained to her bed, skin and bones and filthy. Those people had tied her there and refused to feed her until she told them where her money was. When Allan got there she hadn't had any food or water for two days, and ended up in the hospital in town for over a month to get her strength back. She was never the same after that and Henry was the only person she trusted.

As far as I know, they never did catch up to those people. Granny lived out there for several more years and was always baking or giving Henry small gifts because she was so grateful. I used to tease him by saying that she was sweet on him. We often wondered why they picked on her – maybe because she was old and lonely. Who knows? Sometimes it is hard to understand what makes people do what they do.

One other time he came home and was visibly upset. I remember it was probably late November; there was snow on the ground already.

"Sarah, do you still have any of the boy's smaller jackets around here and maybe some other clothes?"

"Why? I'm sure if I look I can find a few things."

"Well, I was up in the hills today close to the reserve and saw smoke coming from the chimney of the old Charles place Naturally I stopped to say hello.

There was a metis woman there with three little boys; the oldest was probably around five, one not more than a baby. They were dirt poor. There was barely any furniture and the boys were dressed in clothes way too small for them. There was one bed, a stove and rickety old table. There were only a few sticks of wood left in her woodpile and the house was cold.

. Henry filled the sleigh with wood and I dug out what I could find including some old baby clothes I had stored away. I didn't have any jackets that small, but I sent along some toys for the boys, some preserves, two loaves of fresh bread, several jars moose meat and some potatoes. I went with him in case she was afraid to let him in.

Evie was her name and she was a really nice lady. Her sister brought her food from the reserve when she came to visit. Evie told me she had moved here to be with her husband, and he had left a couple of months ago and hadn't come back. She told me that if he wasn't back by spring she was going to take her boys and leave."

Another time I asked him "Did you ever find out her last name?"

"It was an Irish name - Mac something. When I was leaving I noticed the wood we took her was nearly gone, so I thought I would take her a load tomorrow so that at least they will be warm." I sent along some more potatoes and fresh eggs for her.

When Henry got back he told me she said to thank you. When she saw the wood she started to cry. "Sarah, if you don't mind I'll keep an eye on her so she has enough wood to get through until spring?"

Then one day in the spring, he came home from town and told me the old Charles place was empty.

"What happened to Evie and her boys?" I asked.

"Apparently her husband came back and left again, taking the youngest with him. Ray was his name. The oldest boy went to live on the reserve with her sister, and she left with the middle one. Nobody seems to know where she went."

My heart broke for her. "That poor woman, I wonder what will happen to her now?"

"I guess we will never know. Nobody seemed to know much about them."

"This bothered him for a long time. Family was important to Henry and he didn't like the idea of splitting the boys up. I have often thought about her and wondered where she ended up.

Henry never hollered at our boys, but when he did, they listened. If he thought they needed to be punished he sent them out to find a willow first. Then they would drop their pants and accept the switching like a man. The smaller willows stung more than the big ones, but the boys never did figure that out. They always came back with the smallest branch they could find.

He treated everyone the same. He said what he had to, and was respected for it. He could barely read or write, but somehow he had a head for figures. He was as honest as the day was long and I don't recall him ever deliberately cheating anybody. The worst thing he did was make and sell moonshine, but then his motives were honest. We needed the money.

When I think back, I remember him getting mad only once or twice. One time it was about Granny Hubert, and the other was the time the boys took the truck to town without asking and put it in the ditch.

The older boys wanted to go to town and Henry told them they had to stay home. After we went to bed, they pushed the old truck out to the road and started it. It was spring and the roads were still icy in spots. If I remember correctly not one of them had a drivers licence or much driving experience.

Well, to make a long story short, they put the truck in the ditch and had to come home and wake up Henry to hitch up the team of horses to pull the truck out. He was furious. The boys weren't allowed to go to town for a month and he worked their butts off.

"That's funny gram. Did they ever try anything like that again?"

"No, once was enough. As soon as they were old enough they bought their own trucks."

Seventeen

Elyse bounced into Sarah's room, "Hi Gram, my you look nice today. What have you done to yourself?"

"I got my hair cut yesterday. Do you like it?" Sarah replied. She still had a head of thick white hair which she wore in a stylish bob around her face.

To Elyse it looked the same, only shorter, but she agreed anyway, "Looks good."

"Come here Elyse," Sarah said," I have something I want to show you. I went through my trunk the other day and came across this. I don't know why I kept it." Sarah was holding a flat, long tin box in her hands. "I forgot I still had this."

Sarah sat down in her chair and opened the box. A slightly musty odor emanated from the box into the room. Elyse saw a few old tarnished medals and many first place ribbons, some attached to large white rosettes, others plain.

"What are they Gram?" Elyse asked taking one of the medals and turning it over and over in her hands."

"I won these at the bench shows usually held at the same time as the local sports days. While the men competed in the ball tournaments we women had contests of our own to see who made the best. We entered pickles, baking, knitting, sewing, quilting, jam, bread – you name it.

Usually there was a panel of three judges who tasted and judged the items, then declared a winner. As you can see I got quite a few. In my later years I was one of the judges. Believe me that was a lot harder than it looked."

"I read about those shows in the history book, Elyse responded. "From what I can gather some women took winning very seriously. The book mentioned that more than one woman left the judging area in tears because she didn't win."

"True enough, but I never took losing that seriously."

"Did Grandpa Henry ever get one for the best moonshine?" Elyse asked with a serious expression on her face.

"No," Sarah replied, just as seriously, "it never lasted long enough to get there."

"There were two sports days we went to every year. The biggest was at Charles Lake on July first. People came from miles around to attend. A smaller one was held in Clarion on the May twenty-fourth long weekend.

"Tell me about them Gram. We have a County fair on July fourth with fireworks, rides and a rodeo."

"Every area and town had a ball team and each year there was a big baseball tournament. Henry and the boys played ball and were one of the best teams in the area. As soon as the snow was gone they went to the pasture and started practicing.

There was an amateur rodeo for the older boys. They had bareback riding races, calf roping, wild horse races, and a greased pig race. Whoever caught the pig got to keep it. Sometimes they used black axel grease and the contestants were filthy when they were finished. Each year the boys tried but never won. All I ended up with was a mess to try and get out of their clothes. Sometimes it was easier to throw them away. I always had them change into their oldest for that race.

For the younger ones there were foot races, gunny sack races, three-legged races, egg carrying races and other games. For the adults there was a dance on the Friday and Saturday evenings and on the first of July a fireworks display. Of course it was nothing like we see today.

We went rain or shine. Some people camped overnight, but Henry always wanted to go home to check on the farm. I packed a big picnic lunch and we left early in the morning and got home late at night. Usually we went for one day, occasionally two, depending upon whether the ball team was winning or not. The bench show was always held on the first day in the hall. Then we would work frantically to have everything cleared out in time for the dance. Sometimes Henry and the boys went the second day and the girls and I stayed home."

"Sounds like fun. What did your kids do to entertain themselves on the farm Gram?"

"It was probably much easier raising children back then as compared to now. They didn't have all those games to play, movies to see, or places to go. My children are forever running someone, somewhere, to do something."

"I know what you mean. My mom was always taking me or one of my brothers some place."

"Here on the farm they made their own fun, after their chores were done of course. When they got home from school they milked the cow, gathered the eggs, fed the pigs and chickens and cleaned out the barn. After supper it was homework and they always went to bed early.

In the fall the boys stayed home from school to help Henry stook the grain for the threshing machine. The girls helped with the cooking and took the meals for the men out to the fields.

They liked to play in the loft of the barn. There was a rope attached to a pulley and they liked to swing on that. Henry told them not a hundred times, but that didn't stop them. One time Mathew fell and broke his arm, but the next day he was right back up there.

Once a month we took them to town. Henry would give each of them a nickel to go to the movie. The nickel was enough for the movies and a treat. While they were there, we did our shopping. The stores always stayed open until nine on Friday night. I especially liked to go to the Ice Cream Shoppe for an orange float."

"What's that Gram, I never heard of it before?"

"They would spoon with vanilla ice cream into a tall glass, and then fill it with orange soda pop, and you ate it with a long spoon." Sarah rolled her eyes, "it was delicious."

Once a week, during the spring and summer Henry and the boys played ball. While they were gone, I taught the girls how to knit and sew. We always seemed to be busy - there was never a dull moment at our house.

The girls and I went to the local baby and wedding showers. Henry dropped us off at the door and then visited with the other men until we were ready to come home. Sometimes he visited a little too much, but always got us home safely."

"Men didn't go to the showers Gram? They do at home."

"Heavens no Elyse, they weren't interest in going to our "hen Parties" and we sure as heck didn't want them there any way.

After we moved to the Hines place someone was always stopping in for a visit, and of course their kids played with ours.

Sarah got out of her chair, lifted the lid of the trunk and placed the tin box back inside. "Those were the best times. Life was so much simpler then," she stated.

Eighteen

Out of the blue one morning Sarah said to Elyse, "you must be getting tired of listening to me talk. What do you do when you aren't here?"

"Don't worry about me Gram. Believe it or not I have a very active social life. Sometimes I feel like I am related to half the town."

Sarah laughed. "You probably are. Around here a person has to be very careful who they talk about"

"Are you serious Gram?"

"Yes, if you go back far enough many of the families are related through marriage."

Then she added, "What you are doing here is very important to me. You brought Ivan back to me. In turn, I hope I am giving you our family history to share with you family. That way, when I am gone, you will still have a connection to each other."

I wonder if Elise knows how happy she has made me by coming here. The worst part was the not knowing whether he was dead or alive. I can die happy now knowing that he had a good life.

Elyse was quiet for several seconds then she said, "Well then, I guess we better get back to work."

"You are right, no using wasting time. Did I ever tell you that you were a slave driver?"

Elyse grinned, "You haven't seen anything yet."

"By the way, how are you and Rachel getting along? Any better?"

"I think she is still very unhappy with me. At present we agree to disagree, if you know what I mean."

Don't worry about that, she will get over it. You do realize don't you that she is only looking out for me."

"I know Gram, but that doesn't make things ay easier."

"Have patience with her Elyse. She is a good person and you couldn't ask for a better friend if you need somebody."

'I don't think that will ever happen, in the meantime where were we? Why don't you tell me about your other children? Each of them must have a story too. Gram I am curious. Were your children born in a hospital?"

"Heavens no girl, that was a luxury we couldn't afford. Back then we got Sally Bauer, the local midwife to come. When our time arrived, we called for Sally and she came prepared to help birth the baby and stay for a day or two, if she could. Summer to fall was a busy time for her, must have been those long cold winters that did it."

Elise laughed. Gram had quite a sense of humour when she let it out.

"Seven boys and three girls, by today's standard is way too many kids. Today people are shocked if someone has more than four. That's considered a big family." Elyse said.

"Back then nearly everyone had that many children. Old Mrs. Bauer had nineteen before she passed away, and they were a lot worse off than we were.

When I look back, I wonder myself how I managed. We didn't intentionally set out to have ten children, things simply worked out that way. I remember I was either pregnant or nursing a baby for a very long time. We were blessed, but at the time I recall feeling sorry for myself. I always nursed the baby as long as I could because that was supposed to stop me from getting pregnant right away, didn't always work though. No matter how many mouths there were to feed, Henry made sure we never went hungry.

Having babies was a natural process. I'm not saying it was easy and didn't hurt, but was just one of those things that happened. It wasn't really a big deal. After Sally left we went back to work, that part didn't stop

. I kept the cradle in the kitchen where it was warm and beside the bed at night. If my milk was good I nursed the baby as long as I could.

"Let me think. Ivan was first, and Joshua was eighteen months younger than him. Jacob was born a year after that, then little Helen, the one who died, then Anna, Rachel, John, Mathew, Samuel and finally Peter, all of them not quite two years apart. I have thirty-five grandchildren and ten, great-grandchildren with more on the way. If I add in your family it is more than that. Henry and I were always proud of how our children turned out. Of course we had our problems, but when I look back, they were nothing compared to what others had to put up with.

Thankfully they weren't all babies at the same time. The older ones helped with the younger one. Henry made the boys help with chores and from the time the girls were big enough, they helped me in the house.

Ivan had already left home and shortly after the war started Joshua joined the army. A recruiter came to town, looking for young men to volunteer. He made the war sound glamorous and fun. Joshua was under age but joined up any way.

I was really mad at both him and Henry. After signing the papers Joshua came home and told his dad. Instead of marching our boy back to town and telling the recruiter Joshua was under age he did nothing.

I asked Henry how he could consent to this.

Joshua was still a child and we needed him here on the farm."

His response was "now mama, take it easy. They boys will be just fine."

That made me mad. I picked up the frying pan, threw it at him and then sat down at the table and cried.

"Sarah, he isn't going alone. Johnny Smith, Allan Brown and Gordie Stevens are going too. They will watch out for each other."

I looked up at Henry and snapped," Every one of them is underage and too young to know what they are doing.

I guess Henry had enough of my carrying one. He sat down at the table beside me and said "Sarah, a man has to do what he is called to do. It breaks my heart to see those boys go, but we got to let them do it." Then he patted me on the shoulder and put on his boots. "Stop crying Sarah. Don't let the boy see you so upset. I'm going down to the barn to check on the cows."

He told me later he went down to the barn and cried. First Ivan and now Joshua, it hurt him deeply to see those boys leave home.

We had a big send-off party for all four of them. When the time came, Henry drove Joshua to town to catch the train. It was better that way. I was too upset go with them.

We got letters from Joshua all the time. After his training, he went to England and then to Italy to fight. At first his letters were light hearted and filled with adventure, but over time they became more serious and sadder. The boys went through hell. All four came home, but they were never the same.

We had a battery operated radio and at six every evening we turned on the war news. At the end of the broadcast, they read out the names of who was killed or hurt and where they were from. Every day I prayed to the Virgin Mary to bring our boys home safely. Some of the other young men from our area didn't come home. Their parents were devastated. All of us hurt for them because we knew the next broadcast could have the names of our sons. There is a memorial in front of the Legion hall with all of the names of those who never made it home again."

Elyse was quiet. *For the first time I realize those names on the War Memorial back home had family who missed and grieved for them.*

"When Joshua returned he was a changed man. He used to be a happy go lucky kind of guy, nothing seemed to bother him. After he got home he just sat on the step, smoked cigarettes and stared. He drank too much, often going into town and not coming home for days.

He never talked much about the war. The one time I asked him he replied," mom I saw terrible things and I killed people. I'm not proud of what I did and I hope God will forgive me." I didn't know what to say when he talked that way."

One evening Henry asked Joshua to go help him in the barn. When they came back hours later, they were both as drunk as skunks. I don't know what took place. They must have talked things through because Joshua started to settle down after that. Even though I asked, Henry never told me a thing.

He went to work for Ralph in the store and later married Ralph's daughter. He and Betty have four children, two boys, and two girls. Joshua was always happiest when he was around people. The farm was too quiet for him, gave him too much time to think.

. Even today he never talks about the war and absolutely refuses to join the Legion. He says that part of his life is over and best forgotten.

Next was Jacob. He was more serious, quieter and liked to keep to himself. He was shot in Italy during the war, that's why he limps some. You can really notice it when he is tired. Today Joshua and Jacob own the Reindeer lodge on the south end of town and recently opened a second motel in Farmington. He was always good with figures that boy.

The local boys were altogether and went through some bad times in Italy. As far as I am concerned Jacob drinks too much, but he seems to be able to keep working. I worry about him..

Next came John. He was a great one for getting the older boys to help, and then he would disappear. He started many fights too, then stood back and let his brother's finish them.

When he was old enough he joined the air force. He ended up in England, and to hear him tell the story one would think he bombed Berlin and stopped Hitler single handed. He does keep us entertained with all of his stories. I am sure most are not true, but he has a way of making you believe they are. When they get drinking him and Joshua fought about the war. The arguments get quite heated sometimes.

When the older boys left fell Mathew stayed home and helped Henry. When he was seventeen he went to work in the winter on Charlie Blaine's cat train hauling freight up north. He got paid two dollars a day plus room and board.

Back then Elyse there were times Henry and I were on opposite sides. The church played a big part in our lives and we were expected to follow the rules: go to mass every Sunday and Holy days, eat no meat on Friday, go to confession once a week and never marry outside of the church.

Divorces happened, but if one or the other remarried they could come to church, but not take the sacraments. That turned many people away from their faith.

I am pretty sure that is why some of my boys fell away from the church. Three of them married protestant girls and the only way to have their marriage recognized was to get remarried in the church- which of course none of them did. I am glad the church has become more open in its views. Back then those views would have saved a lot of heartache.

Each time Henry tried to talk them out of their decision, there were hard feelings on both sides. I know of families who disowned their child because they married a catholic. They were considered to be ''living in sin." At other times, parents refused to attend weddings – it was a sad time for all of us.

A few days before Mathews wedding I overheard him and Henry going at it. I heard Henry tell him, "If you go through with this you are no longer a son of mine," to which Mathew replied, "fine with me. We are getting married on Saturday whether you like it or not. I am old enough to make my own decisions."

There were a few more angry words then Mathew got into his truck and drove out of the yard. Henry came stomping into the house – one of the rare times I have seen him that angry. I let him rant and rave for a few minutes and then I told him, "Henry Walker you stop right now" Surprisingly he did.

Then I pressed it further and asked, what is the matter with you? Are you willing to lose your son and maybe his children over something like this? That is what is going to happen."

He got a funny look on his face, and was quiet for a long time.

I said him, "the heart can't help who it falls in love with. It doesn't stop to consider religious barriers and what other people may think."

"But mama, the church tells us it is a sin." He replied

Again I said to him, "Mathew is a grown man and quite capable of making his own decisions. If you continue on like this, you will lose your son and divide our family. Is that what you want? Your other children will follow your lead."

"Sarah, are you trying to tell me you agree with what he is doing?"

I took his hand in mine, "No Henry, I don't agree. I feel the same as you do but I'm not going to say anything and I will welcome Ardith into our home as I have the others."

I had a hand stitched picture hanging on the wall. Pointing to it I said," read that to me."

Henry looked at me as if I had lost it. "Love one another as I have loved you."

Then I said look at that saying again and tell me where it says "but only if they are the same religion as I am?"

Henry stared at me. "You are right Sarah. He is

my son, and I am proud of the man he has become. Ardith is the perfect wife for him."

"Henry, that saying is one of God's commandment, the rules of the church are made by men. You need to go to Mathew and agree to disagree, and then speak no more of what you said to each other today.

"That is so sad," Elyse said. "Were Mathew and Henry able to make up?"

"Henry did go to him before the wedding, but I'm not sure what was said. Both were deeply hurt, but in time they forgave each other. After a few years it wasn't important any more.

I was deeply disappointed in both of them but never let it show. I would have gone behind Henry's back if I had to, Mathew was my son too."

"Wow gram, I had no idea things like this went on. Today everything is so different, and I don't know if it really matters anymore, fewer people are getting married. They choose to live together."

"That was a hard time for all of us but we got through it. That's what families do. In spite of their differences, each should be there for the other.

Elyse was quiet. *I wish Grandpa Ivan had tried harder to get in touch with his family. He missed so much.*

"Where was I?" Sarah asked. "Oh yes, I was telling you about the children. Helen, our first little girl, died in my arms from the whooping cough. I still miss her. I often wonder what kind of woman she would have turned out to be.

. Little Anna was a different story. It was April, calving time and we had a late heavy snow storm. I think the cows were all done except for two. One was a heifer and this was her first calf.

Anyway the cow got into trouble. Henry and the boys were in the barn pulling the calf and I needed something from the cellar for supper. The stairs were steep, and I tripped going down and fell to the bottom. I was shaken up but was fine, nothing seemed to be broken. My due date was June.

After we went to bed I woke Henry up and told him go get Sally Bauer. I knew the baby was coming but it was too early."

Henry was out of bed in a flash. I didn't know he could move so fast. Sally lived four miles south of our place. He left on horseback in the snow and it seemed to take forever until I heard Sally's wagon come into the yard. Henry was driving, his horse tied behind,

By the time Sally arrived I was well on my way to having the baby. I was so scared. Helen had died less than a year before and I was afraid I would lose this baby too. My little girl, Anna was born about two hours later and weighed three pounds. She was so tiny that Henry could hold her in the palm of one of his big hands.

I was determined I wasn't going to lose another little girl and vowed to do whatever was necessary to keep her alive. Being so tiny she couldn't suck very well. It just played her out. For the first few days I fed her my breast milk every hour with an eye dropper, just like you would a new born kitten. I kept her in a covered cradle beside the stove to keep her warm. Most of the time, I wrapped her tight and carried her in a sling next to my chest.

At first we didn't know what was going to happen, but after a day or two she began nursing for longer periods of time and started to grow. She was a little fighter that one, and still is. It's hard to believe now that she was once so small. From the time she could walk she followed the boys around, and they spoiled her by giving her everything she asked for.

We are all protective of her, especially Joshua. He used to sit beside her cradle and sing her little songs he made up. When she got older the boys teased her until she cried.

I remember her first date with Timmy Holt. He had his dad's car and was coming to take her to a movie in town. When he got here, all the boys were lined up by the door waiting for him. Poor guy. They scared him so badly he could barely talk. Anna was furious. She did well in school and went to the city to become a Nurse. Today she is the Director of

Nursing here at the hospital.

* * *

"Mom, it's me Jacob, I am here, and so is Mathew. Hang in there for us. Dr. Fred has the results of your tests, now we will find out what you are up against." I heard Jacob speak to another person in the room. "What are you going to tell us?"

"I am afraid the news is not good. She has had a massive stroke, her left side is completely paralysed and most likely she will never regain use of her arm or leg. She is also developing a fever and I am worried she may get pneumonia on top of this. Her chest sounds are rattily.

We can start her on antibiotics. I have already started her on blood thinners to break up the clot, but right now this is a waiting game. We have two alternatives, we can keep her on IV and keep her comfortable or we can take very aggressive action, but I can't guarantee the results. Why don't all of you talk this over and decide, keeping in mind that either way you are not going to have the mother you are used to."

I lay there listening to the silence and the murmur of voices. Then I heard Mathew say with a quiver in his voice.

"She wouldn't want to live the rest of her life like

this. All we ask is that you keep her comfortable and out of pain. We don't want to see her suffer.

Mom can you hear me? Forgive us if we have made the wrong decision. We don't want to lose you but we can't bear to see you linger like this for a long time.

Mathew my strong level headed son, you are doing the right thing. Remember we talked about this when your father died. I told you then I never wanted to suffer like he did. I wish there was some way I could let you know that I approve.

* * *

"Don't ever tell Rachel I said this, but she should have been born a boy. She followed Mathew or Henry like a shadow. Whatever they did, she tried to do.

One time she had a pet pig named Lizzy that she raised from a baby. One day Lizzie stepped into a hole and broke her leg. We had no way of fixing it so Henry shot her. You should have seen Rachel carry on. She refused to talk to Henry for weeks. That winter, every time we had pork for supper she ran to her room crying "I'm not eating Lizzy and you can't make me."

She could shoot, hunt and work like any man and drink with the best of them too. Her first two husbands couldn't handle her life style. Tony settled her down after they got married. I am pretty sure it was because they liked to do the same things. They camped and fished in the summer often bringing me back fresh salmon or tuna. Sometimes I can't believe it is the same girl.

She used to cuss with the best of them, but I notice now she is using a better choice of words most times. She doesn't live that far away so she stops every day to see if I need anything in town or to take me for my appointments, probably her way of checking up on me.

John, the fourth boy was always hard to handle. From the time he was little he was in and out of trouble. I remember one time taking him to the store and he wanted a blue truck. I told him no, that we couldn't afford to buy it.

On the way home, I heard him playing and making truck noises. I turned around to see he had taken the truck from the store. I asked Henry to turn around and made John take that truck back into the store and apologize. The whole episode didn't faze him one bit.

He was always looking for a way to make a fast dollar. He borrowed from the boys, and then would forget to pay them back. After a while they refused to give him any money. How he and Henry would fight. Usually John wanted money, Henry would refuse to give him any, and they would go at it. In the end Henry always ended up telling him to go get a job like the rest.

One time he left after such a fight, the next we heard he was in jail for writing bad cheques. After that he didn't come home very much.

Early one morning the police came to the door to tell us he had been killed in a car accident on his way home from work. We knew he was married and had a daughter, but we hadn't met them yet.

Henry was devastated. We were already living in town and Henry wanted to wait until the rest of the family was up before he told them. We sat there at the table crying and talking, but mostly Henry stared straight ahead, not saying much. Finally around seven he phoned Joshua and told him.

It was really hard on them boys when John got killed. They were often upset with him, but they weren't prepared for one of their brothers not to be there. Those boys were actually quite close, always looking out for the other. They would fight among themselves, but Lord help anyone who picked on one of them.

Henry never got over losing John. After that he often said, "No father should have to bury his son. It should have been me first." I understood how he felt because that was the same way I felt about Helen.

Three months after that we celebrated our fiftieth wedding anniversary. We missed John terribly, but his wife and daughter agreed to come. I still keep in close contact with both of them.

Samuel was the first baby born in the Hospital. That boy was always reading. After he finished his chores he would disappear and Henry usually found him in the loft of the barn reading a book.

He was quieter than the others, never much of drinker and went on to study Agriculture in college. When we decided to move to town, he bought the farm. He uses all of the scientific methods and seems to be doing well today.

Peter was our afterthought baby. I was sure I was getting too old to have babies when he was born. My children were having their own children by then. In fact Peter and his nephew are only a month apart.

When he was little, every one of us pampered him. That child couldn't do anything wrong in our eyes. As soon as he was old enough to drive, he bought a gravel truck and went to work with Mathew. When he was twenty he branched out on his own. He went into the oil patch with his truck and put in many long hard hours. Today he has a big trucking company called Eagle Transport. The other day he was in Calgary, signing some papers to move an oil rig to Texas. Sometimes I think he has been the luckiest of the bunch."

Sarah chuckled. "Oh Lord, some of the things those boys did! Of course it was all in fun, they never deliberately set out to hurt anyone - like the time Joseph's daughter Amanda was getting married. Her wedding dance was held at Miller's hall, about ten miles north of town.

Along about midnight, the police showed up and started handing out illegal possession tickets for having open liquor in cars or drinking outside. In those days that is what you did, none of this buying tickets and drinking in the halls.

Jacob came out and asked them to stop. One officer was willing to leave, but the other got kind of snooty and said he could hand out tickets if he wanted to.

Then the other boys followed Jacob outside to see what was going on. The two officers jumped into their car and radioed for help. The boys started rocking the car, and before you knew it, the police car was nearly on its side. When the boys stopped the police took off out of there as fast as they could. Nobody bothered us for the rest of the night. It was a good thing the officers knew Henry, or there would have been hell to pay. As it was, the boys had to pay for the damages to the car.

A least once a day one or the other of them stopped by. When Henry died, I had quite a time convincing them I could look after myself. Now that they are getting older they have quietened down some.

When we have a family reunion I like to sit back

and listen to the stories. Often, that is when I find out the truth about some things. Of course they still have their disagreements which is only natural, but they are still close and always look out for one another. I thought their antics were going to be the death of me with.. Henry didn't get too excited though.

To me, learning to read and write was important. Soon after we moved here, Mr. Hardy donated land for a school. One winter the men cut and piled extra logs and stacked them at the school site. That spring, after seeding, they built a one room school which went from grade one to nine. Some of the building is still standing at the Cross Road corner.

The men built desks for the children. We pooled our money and Ralph got us a good deal on a blackboard. Millie Weiss was the first teacher. She married Joey Poole and lived in the school yard. Bill Schanter donated the school bell, and the boys took turns ringing it every morning.   In the winter Jim Brown got up early and picked up the kids for school in his sleigh. He added walls and roof and had built benches along the insides. In the summer they walked. I have heard more than one tell their children they walked five miles uphill both ways.

Most of the kids never got past grade nine. In the spring and fall the boys stayed home from school and helped on the farm. The girls went unless they were needed to help at home.

The older boys hated school and most quit before grade seven. Samuel and Peter went to school in town, by then there was a school bus that picked them up.

Clarion was much smaller then. There was Ralph's general store, a post office, livery stable and blacksmith shop, Ford garage, two farm dealerships, two hotels, one with a cafe, the police and railroad station and two churches, one Catholic, the other Presbyterian. I think there were about twenty families living in town back then.

In the 40's Henry worked for a Co-operative that built two grain elevators. Too bad they were torn down years ago. When the passenger train stopped running, the old station was sold and moved away. You probably saw that it is used for the museum today. Sometimes, I worked at the local post office and General store when they needed help. Henry never approved of women working outside the home.

Everybody knew everybody's business, which was not always a good thing. Still seems that way today even though the town is much bigger.

On Saturday night, the boys would head for town. Henry had a rule," if you can party at night you can get up for church in the morning. Many were the times they got home in time to wash up, turn around and come to mass. Often they were a sorry looking bunch.

Each weekend there was a dance somewhere. First they spent the evening drinking at the hotel bar then head out to the dance. After that, there was usually a party at someone's house. Many were the time they ended up at our place, and I got up in the middle of the night and cooked sausage for them. The boys would drift out to the bunk house and go to bed, and then it was left up to me to get their friends out the door, and on their way home. Henry often complained about the noise, but I quite enjoyed them coming. The young ladies were good about helping me clean up before they left.

I remember one time they were upset with Joe Flaraty. He had tried to beat Henry out of twenty dollars. He had Henry fix the hitch on his tractor, used it all spring and then refused to pay. He said it wasn't done right.

One night old Joe was in the bar, and his truck was parked in front. Two of the boys, I think it was John and Mathew, decided to get even with him. They went to Ellie Hanson's and borrowed her goat, then put it in the cab of Joe's truck. When old Joe went to go home, the goat jumped out. It had eaten his seats and the cab of the truck stunk to high heaven.

He came back into the bar cursing and swearing. "If he ever caught the so and so who put the goat in his truck, he would kill them with his bare hands." I imagine my boys looked as innocent as possible. I honestly don't know if Joe ever found out who did it.

Another time John was in the hospital. He had cut his fingers on a saw and Doc. Grant wanted to keep him for a few days in case there was an infection. Well, those boys decided if John couldn't come to the party, they would take the party to him.

Visiting hours were from seven until eight in the evening so one at a time, the boys drifted into John's room. Adelaide Summer was the nurse on duty that evening. Soon she heard a lot of noise coming from behind John's closed door.

Here those boys had taken a jug of Henry's moonshine, and were sitting there drinking it straight. Old Harry Farmer was in the same room as John, and he was as drunk as a skunk and the boys weren't far behind. He must have been nearly eighty then.

Later Adelaide told me it took some doing but she finally got them out of there and then had to look after two very drunk patients. It wasn't that funny at the time, but every time she sees one of them, she tells that story over.

Outside of all this tom foolery they were hard workers. When they left home and began raising their own families, they did what they had to do to put food on the table. In their own way each one of them has been very successful. They all turned out to be good people and I am proud of them today."

Nineteen

"Can I tell you something Elyse that I have never told a soul?"

"Sure Gram, I promise not to tell anyone."

"I have never quite forgiven Henry for buying our house in town."

"Why? Didn't you want to move?"

"No. One day he walked into the house and told me I could start packing,

I looked at him and asked "what are you talking about." I wasn't planning on going any place.

He got a funny look on his face, and then looked down at his shoes. Each time he did that I knew he had done something I wasn't going to like. It was then he announced he had bought a house in town.

I was shocked and angry. "You what?" I yelled at him. "How could you do that with consulting me or asking if I wanted to move to town?"

He looked at me and quietly said "I knew you wouldn't agree, but neither one of us are getting any younger. I think it's time one of the boys took over the farm. Everything will be just fine,"

How I hated it when he would say that to me. He was always doing things like that then telling me after the fact. How did he know any of the boys wanted the farm in the first place?   I found out later that he had talked to them about his idea and they agreed it was time for us to move off the farm. His mind was made up, and no matter what I said, he wasn't about to change it.

That was one of the few times I was spitting mad at him. I wish he would have talked it over with me first. If we were going to move to town that wasn't the house I would have bought. I still get angry when I think about that day.

Elyse didn't know what to say. "You never told your girls how you felt?"

Abruptly Sarah replied. "They don't need to know. What was done was done." Henry had bought that ugly green house on the corner of Elm and Pine and, at first, I hated being in town. There was nothing but noise, horns honking, cars coming and going all hours of the night. I missed the peace and quiet of the farm. I missed hearing the birds sing in the morning and the drone of the bugs. The farm was our home for over thirty years and, for some of us, sometimes change is hard.

In my heart I don't think he wanted to move either, but the chores and looking after the cattle were getting to be too much. Time was passing by. In the, end the move turned out to be the right thing to do.

I think one of his reasons he decided to move was that his back was giving out. All those years of hard work finally caught up to him. He was in pain most of the time, but didn't let me see how much.

He drove out to the farm every day to see how things were going and to help if he could. I am sure he missed the place more than he let on. Sunday was his favourite day. Usually one of the boys would stop by and the cards would come out.

At least our new home had room for a garden, although it was much smaller than the one on the farm. I still planted fresh vegetable like lettuce, radishes, onions, pea, beans, and tomatoes, the kind of things I could pick and use for a meal. For the first couple of years, we planted the potatoes, carrots, turnips, cabbage, at the farm. Henry built me a cold room in the basement so we could keep the vegetable all winter, but it wasn't as good as the root cellar at home.

There were raspberry bushes, rhubarb plants and a strawberry bed which was good to have. When we moved there, that garden spot was such mess it took most the first summer to get it cleaned up and producing again. I didn't have to do all that work, but fresh always tasted better than that stuff we could buy at the store.

I still made bread twice a week which was now easier with my electric stove. When we first moved, the kids bought us a washer and dryer. From spring to fall, I hung the clothes outside, but in the winter I used the dryer. Nothing beats climbing into a bed with fresh sheets that dried in the open air.

I made myself get used to living in town. I wasn't much for going out and joining things. I preferred to stay at home. Once a month, Harriet Brown would pick me up and take me to the Ladies Aid meeting. I'm still a member, but quit going after I had my stroke.

"Didn't you get lonely?" Elyse asked.

"Oh no child, why would you think that? Just about every day someone stopped by for tea. The kids or grandkids often popped in at meal time. The neighbors usually stopped when they were in town. We always had lots of company."

I liked having the church two blocks away. Henry and I walked to mass every morning. He usually stayed to have coffee with Father Leo, and often brought him back for lunch. They had some fairly lively discussions about what was going on in the world. If Henry got loud, Father Leo got louder.

Henry settled in faster than I did. One day I told him he was turning into a nosey busybody since moving to town. He seemed to know everything that is going on. He turned red and didn't say a thing.

I used to tease him about making his rounds every day to check up on people. First he went to the post office, and then the grocery store. Sometimes he stopped in to visit the boys. If it was a Friday afternoon they insisted he stay for what they called a "safety meeting" which was an excuse to have a drink. I don't know how many times one or the other brought him home a little tipsy."

"I wish I had been able to get to know him, He sounds like a real character."

Sarah chuckled. "Yes, at times he was."

"Grandpa Ivan was a lot like him by the sounds of it. He was loud and boisterous too. I had people tell me they were afraid of him the first time they met him Yet, if someone needed help he would have given them the shirt off his back."

Sarah became quiet. When Elyse looked over she could see a smile on her face and it was as though she was lost in the past.

Seconds later Sarah sighed and began talking again. "For quite a few years Henry babysat at the jail. If the RCMP had someone in custody, he sat with them at night until they were either released or transferred to Farmington. He always gave the young boys a lecture about smartening up and making something out of their lives. Not one of them held a grudge afterward. Not only did he know everybody in town they knew him. Sometimes the police brought him home on a Friday night instead of letting him drive. He thought nothing of calling them up and asking for a ride, like they were his own private taxi service.

"That wouldn't happen today. You would be arrested for being drunk and disorderly."

"I think that would have happened if somebody other than Henry called. They had a soft spot for him. Besides if they put Henry in jail, who would babysit him until morning?"

"I never thought of that Gram. That's funny."

"Every spring and fall he would do what he could to help Jacob on the farm. He had his still out there and every now and then ran off a batch of moonshine. His job was to drive the grain truck for the boys when they were harvesting. We still butchered our meat there. Every fall we put a half of beef and a whole pig into the deep freeze and I still canned about three hundred jars of vegetables, fruit, jam and jelly.

Henry would say to me, "why do you work so hard in that garden? I can buy all we need at the store."

"Henry," I would say back to him. 'What am I going to do with myself if I don't do this? I have done it all my life."

Henry always stopped along the road on his way home and picked berries for me, and Millie Brown brought us fresh cream and eggs every Saturday.

He had a weakness for auction sales. Every time

he went, he brought homes boxes of junk. He couldn't resist a bargain and he always had an excuse "I thought Jacob could use it" and then take the box down to the basement. Every once in a while I would go through the boxes, keep what was good and throw the rest away. Half of the time, I don't think he even knew what he bought, and I would get tired of having all of that junk in my basement.

Each fall Mathew would go moose hunting and he and Henry would make most of it into moose sausage. That was quite a production and kept Henry busy for days. First he spent better part of two days making sure the basement and tools were clean. First he would go to the butcher shop and have them grind the meat, buy the casings and then he would buy enough ground pork and fat to mix with the moose meat. There was a certain formula he followed. In the old days, on the farm I spent hours washing and scraping the intestines of the pigs to make the casings for him.

Nest he put all of the meat and spices in a galvanized wash tub and mixed it with his hands. When he thought it felt right, he would smell the mixture and then bring a little upstairs for me to cook. When he decided it tasted right, one of the boys would stuff the meat into the sausage stuffer, and Henry's job was to feed on the casing. It had to be stuffed just enough so that the casing was full, but not enough to break it. He would twist the sausage in a certain way and when that casing ran out put the sausage into another washtub.

Of course the more sausage they made, the more beer they drank. Then the stories would really start to fly. Most times, before they finished, more people would show up to help and it got to be quite a party. My job was to cook enough raw sausage to give everybody a taste. Since he passed the kids have tried, but it never tastes exactly like what Henry used to make.

He insisted on bringing the smoke house with him when we moved here. I told him town was no place for a smoke house, but of course he didn't listen. He still smoked our hams and turkeys and of course the moose sausage every fall.

One time he just about lost it all. He lit the smoke house and went to get the mail. I heard the fire engines come up the alley and then stop. I ran outside just in time to stop them from turning the water onto the smoke house. Seems old granny Peterson next door saw the smoke, thought it was a fire, and called the fire department. It took me some time to convince them there was no fire, that Henry was only smoking meat.

He came home while the fire truck was still there and I will never forget how upset he was. He kept muttering something about "old busy bodies should mind their own business" Thankfully the meat was saved that day. I recall telling the firemen to come back the next day and I would give them some. After that day he and Joshua moved it back to the farm.

I used to wonder what our life would have been like if we had stayed in Alton. We probably would have been like my brother and cousin who ended up losing their farm and living off the money from the government. They went through some tough times after we left.

It was hard for him when he got the cancer, but he never complained. He simply said "this is God's will. I have had a good life and, if my time is up, I am ready."

We had only been in town for six years when Henry got sick. He started by complaining he wasn't feeling well and couldn't eat. I started to get worried when he began losing weight.

I would say to him, "Henry you get yourself down to see Doc. Flynn and find out what is wrong. You are barely eating enough to keep a bird alive."

He would tell me, "everything is fine mama, you worry too much."

Then one morning he decided to stay home instead of coming to church with me. All he said was "I don't feel good today, must have a touch of the flu."

When I got back he was throwing up blood and

asked me to make an appointment for him. I phoned Anna and we took him to emergency right away. They put him into the hospital that same day for tests, but in the end it was the cancer.

He fought hard. He tried chemo therapy, but that just made him sicker. After a while, he refused any more treatment and was gone in three months. I begged him to keep on with his treatments; I wasn't ready to lose him yet. It broke my heart to see my big strong Henry reduced to a mere shadow of himself.

We kept him home for as long as we could, but finally had to put him into the hospital. That was hard on all of us, especially him. He hated his kids hovering over him, and hated having to ask someone to help him go to the bathroom. All his life he had done everything for himself.

One time he insisted on coming back home. That lasted for a few days and then I had to take him back. The last time he went into the hospital the children and I took turns staying with him day and night. Father Leo came every day to give him communion

One evening, when I was the only one sitting with him, he looked at me and said "Sarah Walker you are an amazing woman to have put up with me all these years. Without you by my side none of this would have been possible. Thank you my love."

Tears were running down his cheeks, his eyes

were filled with pain. It was unusual for him to say things like that because he wasn't a sentimental man. I always knew he loved me, but he wasn't one to say it out loud.

I called in the nurse and she gave him an injection that she said would help. Usually he teased her, but this evening he was silent. After a while he drifted off to sleep, and I sat there holding his hand.

At one time he opened his eyes, looked at me and said "mama you go home now. You look tired. I will see you tomorrow." I should have been able to see what he was doing. He was saying goodbye to me.

I was tired and against my better judgment went home. Before I left I leaned over and whispered in his ear. "I love you Henry, always did, always will. I'll be back in the morning."

Even though his eyes were closed he answered clearly "I love you too Sarah." Those were the last words he said to me.

I stayed for a few more minutes then left. He went to sleep and never woke up again. He was never alone after that. We took turns staying with him. I'm not sure if he knew we were there, but I like to think he did. After about ten days, he just drifted away from us and was gone.

Sarah's eyes filled with tears. Elyse reached over, took one of her hands and squeezed it tight. She felt like crying too. "That was the same way as Grandpa Ivan. One of us was always with him, but it was you he wanted."

Sarah reached over to the side table and pulled a handful of tissues from the box. Dabbing at her eyes she replied, "I wish I could have been there but now do you understand why I wasn't?"

"Yes Gram. I wish I had known about the picture beforehand. Maybe I might have been able to find you sooner."

"Wasn't meant to be that way child," Sarah said and then continued with her story. "Fifty five years of loving and living with someone doesn`t go away overnight and is never enough. In fact, it took me quite a while. I was lonely most of the time. People came and went as usual, but it was different. Father Leo was very good. I think he missed Henry as much as I did, maybe even more.

One of the kids stopped by every day. I think they were worried about me. I don't remember much during that time and what I do is fuzzy. To this day, no matter how hard I try, I still can't recall most of what went on.

I didn't sleep well. I was used to having Henry beside me and I hated being alone. Sometimes, when it was really bad, I would prop pillows under the covers, curl up against them and pretend it was my Henry laying there.

After a year I decided to sell the house and began going through things. So many memories. If I thought one of the children would like something particular I put their name on it. Lots of stuff wasn't worth keeping so I donated it or threw it into the garbage. Everyone who had given me a certain gift, I gave back to them. The hardest part was keeping it even. Nothing causes more hard feelings than one thinking they got less than the others. I feel badly that I have nothing of Ivan's to give you. I am sorry Elyse. What little he left behind disappeared years ago."

"No problem Gram, I understand. You didn't know he was still alive."

"When I was finished, I phoned the children to come for supper, just them; no wives, husbands or grandchildren. When we finished eating I told them "I want to sell the house and move into one of those new seniors' condos that are being built.

I have a list of furniture I want to take with me. I have also put your names on items I thought you would like to have and on anything you gave me. Everything else in the house is to go to an auction sale. If there is more that you want, you will have to buy it at the sale."

Henry and I still had most of the money from selling the farm invested in the bank. That day I gave each of them a cheque for $15,000. I thought this way there would be no fighting. I have seen too many families fall apart when the last parent dies.

Anna tried to talk me out of giving them the money. "Mom, keep your money, you may need it."

"No, Anna I won't." I told her. "All I need is a roof over my head and enough to eat. I have enough left to pay for the condo and my funeral. One thing I do ask of all of you is to make sure my wedding cross goes to the eldest child's family and continue to be passed down."

Joshua got very upset and tried to talk me out of doing this. "You should stay here in the house, keep the money and think for a while longer before you make any rash decisions."

I looked at him and said "one day you will be old too. Then you get to decide what is right or wrong. I have decided this is what I am going to do, and I don't want to hear any more." I don't think he liked that, but my mind was made up.

I got a good price for the house. You know Elyse, I worked hard all my life. I just wanted a little place I could relax and enjoy. I wanted to spend time with my family and not be bothered trying to keep up a garden and such. Besides, I wanted to do this while I still had my wits about me."

Elyse could picture Gram saying this to Joshua. She would have had her hands on her hips, looking up at him, her eyes sparkling as she told him what she thought. She giggled.

"Poor old Joshua didn't know what to say. None of them were happy, but eventually they came around to my way of thinking. Had to because I wasn't about to change my mind.

I never did get to move into that condo. I had my first stroke and we all decided it would be better if I moved here, into the lodge. I have my own room, three meals a day and a roof over my head, and the staff is very good to me. That's all I need.

Sometimes their parents leave my great-grandchildren with me for a few minutes while they parents shop and we have tea. I keep chocolate covered marshmallow cookies for them and we use real tea cups with milk and sugar. They look forward to those times and are always asking to hear stories about the olden times.

When my girls were small, and there were no men around, we used to sit around the table and have tea and cookies. That was our girl time. Often life was so busy that the girls were treated just like the boys. This gave us that special time to be girls and talk about female things. The best part is now I get to do the same thing with my great-granddaughters."

Twenty

"Gram I can't believe how hard you had to work all the time," Elyse exclaimed. "I know for a fact I would have had a hard time keeping up to you."

Sarah laughed. "Why would you think that? Life was a whole lot simpler then than it is now. You young people lead very complicated lives."

Sarah tried to laugh again, but ended up coughing so hard she could barely catch her breath. Elyse got up, reached for the glass of water sitting on the end table and held it up to her lips. After several small sips, Sarah leaned her head back against the couch. She was exhausted.

"Gram, this is too much for you today. Guess what? I'm going to give you a day off."

"Elyse, I am fine. Go fetch us some tea and put honey in mine. Soothes the throat you know. All of this coughing takes my breath away, but I'll be ready to talk again in a few minutes."

Elyse went down the hallway to the common area, made two cups of tea and brought them back to Sarah's room. Gram was sitting with her head back and her eyes closed.

It's plain to see Gram isn't getting over her cold. Each day she looks more fragile than the day before. This is the first time I have noticed that her color is poor. She is pale with a dusky tinge to it. Maybe this wasn't such a good idea. Maybe all of this is wearing her out. I've only been thinking about myself up until now. Not once have I thought of how taxing this must be on her.

She recalled that when she had arrived her reasons were selfish. She wanted to know more about the people who had ignored her grandfather, but now it was much more than that. She was finding and getting to know about family she never knew existed. The pages for the book she was writing were piling up on her desk

Now things are different. This family has taken me in as one of their own. They've invited me for meals, regaled me with stories of their childhood, many of which are now part of my story.

Her initial anger and reluctance had given away to acceptance and love. She wished she had gotten to meet Grandpa Henry. She adored Gram.

"Gram, you rest today," she said placing the cup of tea in front of her. "I just remembered I have something I need to do. Is anyone coming over later?"

"Yes, Anna is coming after lunch."

"Good. I don't think you should be alone all the

time." Kissing her on the cheek Elyse said, "Tomorrow, same time, and same place?"

"I'm not going anywhere," Gram replied in a teasing manner. "I'll be here."

As soon as Elyse closed the door and began walking down the hallway, the tears she had been holding back began to flow. She wiped them from her eyes and made a decision. *I am going to find Rachel and tell her I am going home in the morning. I have been so unfair to Gram.*

With the music blaring from her car stereo, she drove the short distance to Rachel's house. As she pulled up in front, she could see Rachel bent over pulling weeds from her flower bed.

"Rachel?" she called out, "Can I stop for a few minutes to talk to you?"

"Sure Elyse. What brings you here today? I didn't hear you drive up."

Elyse got out of her car and walked over to where she was standing. "Rachel, Gram is getting sicker isn't she? Tell me the truth please."

Hearing the fear in Elyse's voice Rachel turned to her and said, "Yes Elyse. She is wearing out. The Doctor says she has Congestive heart failure. That means her heart is failing and her lungs are filling with fluid. That's part of the reason she is coughing these days. We simply have to wait and see what happens, and how well she responds to her new medication."

Elyse looked into Rachel's eyes. "I have been so selfish. I only thought about me and what I wanted to know about grandfather's family, I didn't think about how hard this would be on her. I am so sorry. I shouldn't have come here in the first place; I should have just left well enough alone."

"Don't be sorry. You're not to blame for any of this Elyse. Mom is old. We have been lucky to have her with us this long." Looking at Elise she continued, "Your coming and being here has done more good than any medicine the Dr. has given her. She knows where Ivan is now and you have told her about his life. She needed to know that he called for her when he was dying. She doesn't have to wonder any longer if he still cared for or had forgotten his family. By coming, you have given her peace. In fact, you have given her a beautiful gift that none of us would have been able to."

"Rachel, I can't stay here any longer. When I first came here, it was because I wanted to get even. I was going to tell you what I thought about all of you and let you know my pain. Now you have become like family to me. I feel like I belong here."

Rather than say anything Rachel let her ramble on. "Every day I feel like a fraud. Gram is sick and here I am pumping her for more information. I'm not angry any more Rachel. I have decided to go home in the morning. Do you think you could you explain that to her for me? I can't."

While talking, they had wandered into the back yard and were now sitting on the white wicker chairs on the patio.

"Stay there Elyse. I'm going to get us some iced tea, and then we'll talk some more."

Rachel went into the house and Elyse stared out over the back yard. It was peaceful and relaxing. Along one fence was a well-tended vegetable garden. At the end of the lot was a large maple tree, its branches bent over, nearly touching the ground. Underneath it was a rock fountain, the water trickling into a small pond. The flower beds along the other fence line were a riot of color, the plants in various stages of bloom. Half barrel wooden planters sat on all four corners of the brick patio with pink and purple flowers cascading down the sides.

Elyse awoke from her reverie when Rachel placed a tray with a pitcher of iced tea, two glasses and a plate of chocolate chip cookies on the wicker table between the chairs.

"You have a beautiful yard Rachel. I could sit here all day and soak in the peacefulness of it."

"Thanks you," Rachel replied. "I have been meaning to cut that huge tree down but I don't have the heart. Anyway, while I was in the house I was doing some thinking, and I personally think you should stay for a while longer."

"But…"

"I understand why you found us. I would be as mad as hell too, but you also need to understand that times were different then. The communications we have today were never even thought of. Most of their information came as word of mouth from a friend or neighbour or by letter that took weeks to arrive. Telegrams were the fastest and usually brought bad news.

If you want to make any sense out of all of this tell her story. Mom is still a brave courageous woman. She didn't have any close neighbours or family to rely on, no modern conveniences, yet managed to build a life and raise a big family. Ivan not returning home was only one of the heartbreaks she endured. Believe me, if she didn't want to be part of what you are doing, she would have said so right from the beginning.

Mom is excited about this. It's as if she has a new purpose for living. Elyse, don't take this away from her. Your leaving now would be like losing Ivan all over again. You are the only link she has to him.

I am sorry I treated you so badly. I was jealous. You and mom had something special, and I wanted to be a part of whatever it was. I convinced myself you were a scam artist and only going to her money. This gave me a reason to doubt and mistrust you. I am so terribly sorry.

"I didn't ask her for anything Rachel."

"I know that now."

Elyse chuckled. "I forgive you." Then laughing she added "Gram and I knew the truth all along so we weren't really worried about what you thought. She had everything all figured out."

"I should have known that," Rachel replied. "She could always figure out what was going on in our heads before we did. It took a lot to fool her. Tony is away so would you like to stay and have supper with me? I'll call Anna to come join us. You need to give yourself time to think before you up and leave."

Later, when Elyse returned to her motel room she felt no closer to making a decision. She threw herself on the bed and cried deep heart wrenching sobs, finally shedding the tears for her grandfather which she had held back for too long. She cried because Gram was very sick and she was going to lose her too.

After a bit she wandered around the room. She made a pot of coffee and while it was brewing she picked up random sheets of paper and read what she had written. When the coffee was ready, she phoned her mother on her cell phone.

When her mother answered the phone Elyse said "Mom, I need to talk to you. I need some advice."

She poured out her story to her mother. "I don't

know what to do. Should I stay? Should I come home? What would you do? What if I lose my job?"

After listening for over half an hour Jean asked her daughter, "Elyse what does your heart tell you? What do you want to do? Honey, if you leave now you will always wonder. If you stay it is possible that Gram may get sicker and pass away. Either way, your heart will be hurt. You are the only one who can make this decision. Whatever you decide, I will support you.

My suggestion is to go to bed, and get some sleep. Things will look different in the morning. Tomorrow is a new day."

"Thanks mom, you are right as usual. Love you."

"Love you too. Goodnight."

Somewhere in the night Elise made the decision to stay, to follow the project to the end, whatever that might be. Between the history books, family stories and conversations with Sarah she had nearly all the information she needed. Leaving would be hard and eventually she would have to go home… just not yet.

Twenty One

The next morning, when Elyse arrived at Sarah's room, she was surprised to find Rachel with her mother. She felt uneasy when Rachel announced, "we have been waiting for you."

Elyse looked at Gram, and said, "We must be going to talk about something serious today if Rachel is here. Do you have a new boyfriend I don't know about?"

Sarah blushed. "Oh Elyse for heaven's sake, There aren't too many men my age around anymore. Shame on you girl! No, we were reminiscing about some of the stranger happenings at the farm. It wasn't all work and no play, we had our moments." Her eyes were twinkling, her voice stronger that it had been for the past several days.

When Sarah looked away Rachel whispered to Elyse, "I take it you have decided to stay a little longer?"

"Yes, I have. Thank you for everything Rachel."

"Rachel," Gram began speaking, "do you

remember the time Chuck and Mirabelle Grayson stopped on their way home from town? They had recently bought their first car. They were so proud of that car and loved showing it off. Every Saturday, on their way home from town, they stopped at our place for a few games of cards.

Anyway, when they stopped this time, Mirabelle came into the house and Chuck walked down to the barn to see Henry. The two of them loved to try and beat us women and Henry had a real knack for remembering who played what card when. He used to holler if you played the wrong suit or led out with the wrong card. Mostly Mirabelle and I ignored his little outbursts. How that man hated to lose a Whist game.

I happened to glance out the kitchen window to see if I could see where the kids were and I noticed a flickering light. "Henry what's that light out there?"

"I lit the garbage pile on fire, it must be reflecting off the windshield of Chuck's car. Chuck, don't you think this would be a good time to check on that fire?"

"Sure do Henry" he replied.

They went outside, but I don't know why they were trying to be so secretive. Mirabelle and I knew what they were up to. They were gone for a long time and when they came back I could tell by the smell they had been testing Henry's latest batch of

Moonshine. They were laughing carrying on like you wouldn't believe and Mirabelle and I were getting upset with their shenanigans.

John came running into the house. "Dad there is a fire outside."

"It's okay John. I lit the garbage pile on fire before supper."

"It's not that dad. The Grayson's car is on fire."

We all ran outside, and sure enough, flames were shooting out of the open back windows. Henry went into action and started shouting orders.

"John, you and the boys go get pails of water and throw it on the grass around the car. Throw some of it into the windows if you can. Chuck, you and I better try to push the car away from the house. We might be able to push it onto the driveway.'

Chuck opened the front door on the driver's side put the car into neutral and together they pushed it backwards into the middle of the yard. The boys were still running back and forth with pails of water throwing them on the burning car. Suddenly there was a whoosh, a boom and the car went flying up into the air and landed upside down.

It was utter chaos. The boys kept throwing water on the fire, Henry and Chuck got two shovels and started shovelling dirt to put out the flames. Mirabelle was howling like a banshee. I finally sent her into the house to make a pot of tea, so I didn't have to listen to her any more.

When all of the excitement seemed to be over I went back into the house. A few minutes later Henry and Chuck came in dirty and black from the smoke.

"You know Henry; I thought there might have been a hole in that Kerosene can. I meant to put in a different one in this morning." Chuck said, as if he didn't have a care in the world. At that Mirabelle started howling again.

The four boys had come into the kitchen and stood by the door, looking down at the floor. It was hard to tell who was who behind them dirty faces.

"Boys," I asked. "Do you have an idea how Mr. Grayson's car caught fire?"

Nobody said anything.

"You better tell us now. If we find out later that you had something to do with it, you will get the licking of your life from your dad."

Finally Timmy Grayson stepped forward. "It's my fault. We had sticks and were playing in the fire. When the tip got red hot we were running around the yard, pretending it was fireworks. I was running around the car and I guess the tip fell in."

"Mine too" said our Johnny. "I was chasing him when that happened. We looked, but we couldn't see anything."

"Now what?" I asked.

The boys hung their heads, Mirabelle was still sniffling in the corner and Henry and Chuck were calmly sitting at the table drinking a beer.

Thank goodness it was one of theirs that started the fire, not one of mine. I don't know what we would have done, if we would have had to pay for that car. I was angry too because those boys knew better.

Chuck and Henry finally figured out what happened. The kerosene can had been leaking on to the back floor mat. Chuck had also bought a jug of moonshine from Henry and put it on the floor beside the kerosene can. The burning tip had fallen through the window and landed on the floor mat filled with kerosene. When the flames got too hot the jug of moonshine exploded. That's what made the car blow up.

Henry drove Chuck, Mirabelle and the boys home in our old car. She was still snivelling when she went out the door.

Later, when we thought about what happened, we realized that if that hot tip had fallen on the dry grass in the yard we could have lost everything. Now it's funny, but it sure wasn't then."

"Mom, tell her about the pigs." Rachel said. "I remember that only too well."

Elyse was giggling, tears running down her face "Gram already told me that one." Then looking at

Sarah she asked. "Was that a true story Gram?"

"You bet it was" she replied, very seriously. Rachel was shaking her head up and down, unable to speak because she was laughing so hard.

"I wish I could have seen that too. I wonder how a pig or chicken know if they have a hangover."

The three of them dissolved into fits of laughter. Each would try to stop, look over at one of the others and start all over again.

Twenty Two

The voices are back, but they seem fainter and further away.

"I shouldn't have taken her for that drive, but she wanted to go so badly. She was waiting for me when I got to her room and insisted I had to see where my grandfather had lived. I checked with the nurse and she thought it would be good for her to get out for a while. She was so excited I couldn't say no.

"Elyse, don't blame yourself for this. She hasn't been well for a long time" said Anna replied, in an attempt to comfort her.

"She told me that she wanted to see the homestead one more time that this would probably be the last time she got out there. I wanted to go too, and it seemed like the right thing to do at the time."

"You had no way of knowing this was going to happen. None of us did. Mom has been asking me for some time to take her, but I always put it off. Lately it seemed like I was always too busy to take time for her. I think you made her very happy. I, for one, am

glad you took the time to take her."

Elyse don't cry. I wanted to take her into my arms and soothe her but my arms wouldn't move. I had been thinking about this ever since you came. When I woke up yesterday I felt stronger than I have for a long time. I thought if I could show you where your grandfather lived that you would understand more about him. Besides I wanted a ride in your convertible, with the top down. That is something I never had a chance to do in my life. My kids thought that because I was old I wouldn't want to experience new things.

* * *

It was a beautiful, warm, summer day, not too hot. A gentle breeze ruffled the leaves of the leaves on the weeping birches in front of the lodge. When Elyse arrived at Sarah's room, she was fully dressed, waiting by the door with her coat and purse.

Before she had a chance to say anything Sarah said," I have a favor to ask. Will you take me out to the homestead? I want to show you where your grandfather lived and our old farm."

"Are you sure you are up to this Gram?"

"Of course, or I wouldn't have asked, and I want the roof down on that car of yours."

"It's called a top Gram, not a roof."

"Do the same jobs don't they?" Sarah huffily replied.

Sarah proceeded to walk out the door. Elyse grabbed the red and black afghan from the back of one of the chairs before following her out.

"Going out are you Mrs. Walker," the receptionist asked.

"Yes, I am going for a ride in my great-granddaughter's convertible with the top down."

"Have a good time girls," she replied winking at Elyse. "How long do you think you will be gone? Will you be back in time for lunch?"

"No, we will be gone for as long as it takes."

"Is it okay to take her for a ride?"

"No problem. It will do Sarah some good to get out of here for a while. She will let you know if she gets too tired and is ready to come back."

They walked down the sidewalk, Sarah steadying herself with her cane, Elyse behind ready to catch her if she stumbled. When they arrived at the car she helped Sarah into the front seat, buckled her seatbelt and tucked the afghan around her legs.

Getting into the driver's seat she said jokingly "Your chariot waits. Where are we going?"

"First we are going to drive around town. I want to show you where Henry and I lived for so many years. Then we will take a drive in the country. I want to show you the area we lived in, although most of the old buildings are gone."

Before leaving town Elyse glanced at the gas gauge. "We won't be going very far unless I put some gas in."

Sarah waited in the car while Elyse filled the car with gas and bought two bottles of water. When she returned she pushed a button and the top began to rise out of the back of the car.

"Stop Elyse, and humor an old lady, leave the roof down. I want to feel the wind on my face. It's been a very long time."

Elyse started to correct her, but when she looked over Sarah was smiling, with an innocent look in her face.

Sarah then reached into the pocket of her coat, pulled out a twenty dollar bill and handed it to Elyse. "I heard once when the girls went on a road trip they shared expenses. Here take this as my share. Don't want it to be said I didn't pay my way."

Giggling like two school girls, Elyse pulled out onto the street.

"Let's go downtown first." Sarah said. Then she added, "wait; there is that stuffy Mrs. Pettigrew. Honk your horn as you pass her."

Elyse did just that. Sarah waved and Mrs. Pettigrew stood there watching the car with a funny look on her face. Like teenagers on a Saturday night they drove up and down Main Street, Elyse honking the horn and Sarah smiling and waving at those who bothered to look. "Too bad you weren't a man Elyse that would give them old girls something to talk about.

Over there, on the corner, is the old house Henry and I lived in until he died. Whoever owns the place now still hasn't painted that ugly green siding. Henry picked the colour, and had .the boys paint it He thought it was perky, but I have always hated it.

Turn at the next corner and follow this road out of town. Over there is the cemetery where Henry and John are buried side by side. There is a place beside them for me too. I had them put my name on the headstone, now all that has to be added is the date I died. It will be easier on the kids that way. One more decision they won't have to make."

"Stop Gram, I don't like to hear you talk that way."

"Don't fret child, I don't have any plans on moving there yet, but I am old and can't live forever. At the end of this road turn right and then follow the road. That will take us to the homestead."

The road was gravel and very dusty. Elyse slowed down and pulled as far to the right as she could each time a car passed. She was worried that a rock would fly up and crack her windshield. She heard that it happened all the time on gravel roads.

Sarah looked out the side window noticing that

the fields they passed were in varying degrees of maturity. Some, still a lush green, others ranging from pale yellow to gold. Cows grazed lazily in the pastures. Spruce and poplar trees lined the sides of the road. The bright blue sky, with a few wispy white clouds contributed to the perfect day for a ride in the country.

Elyse drove slowly and Sarah pointed out the various landmarks – who lived where, and small bits of gossip involving the same people.

"Elyse, when you read the history books, I want you to realize those names stand for real people. They were my friends and neighbours, and some lived very hard lives.

Turn into the next driveway Elyse, this is the place we bought from Minnie Hines. Joshua still lives here, but I see nobody is home."

Pointing at an empty spot she continued, "That was where our old house used to stand. Joshua tore it down quite a few years ago, said it was a fire hazard. See that old Maple tree? I planted that the same year we moved here.

Minnie named this place Blue Hawk and we never bothered taking the sign off the barn Why I don't know. Henry and the boys spent one whole summer building that machine shed you see at the end of the driveway. It kept them busy and out of trouble that's for sure.

We can turn around here. See that old pile of wood across the road? That's where Henry kept his still, and where the pigs and chickens got so drunk. Funniest thing I ever saw.

Elyse turned around and stopped at the end of the driveway. "Which way now Gram?" she asked.

"Turn right here," Sarah replied, "go to the third road and then turn right again."

Elyse did as she was told, but the road ended in an empty field. She looked at Sarah kind of puzzled. "There is nothing here."

"Drive over to that far stand of trees, just ahead of you. That's where we lived when we first moved into this part of the country."

Carefully Elyse followed a barely discernible track across the field "I hope I don't run over anything or hit a rock and take the oil pan off. We would have a long walk home." she joked. Fortunately the ground was fairly even and she could clearly see there were no obstacles in her path. *Mustang convertibles are not made for this.*

Nestled back in the trees was an old log house. Sarah felt a twinge of regret when she saw the door hanging on one hinge, all the windows were broken, and there was a huge hole in the roof. Someone had added an addition to the side. Surprisingly the logs appeared to still be in good shape.

"Doesn't look much different than when I first

saw it, except for the hole in the roof. I was some upset with Henry for not making sure the house was livable, but we managed to make this our home.

Pointing to the left Sarah added, "Over there is where my garden used to be. Look you can still see part of the fence we had around it to keep the pigs out. Each time those they got loose those pesky pigs decided my garden was a delicious treat.

I used to have roses planted along the front of the house, and this field was filled with colourful wild flowers. If you walk straight ahead, to the back of the house, you will come to the creek we used for water. Over there was the blacksmith shed. Henry took it down and moved it to the Hines place. He said it was too good to leave behind."

Elyse reached over, opened the glove compartment and took out her camera. She got out of the car and took pictures of each building. *There really isn't much to see but I think she understands it means a lot for me to be here.*

" Come on Elyse, let's go. The day is wasting. There is more I want to show you."

Back on the main highway they had barely travelled a mile when Sarah asked Elyse to pull over and stop.

"This intersection is what was known as Four Corners. On one corner was the school, and across from it was the hall, picnic grounds and ball diamonds. We had a lot of good times there. On that corner were the post office and store and the church stood across from it. The cemetery where we buried Helen is behind the church. Do you think we could try and drive in there?"

Elyse looked and quickly picked out a faint trail visible through the tall grass which indicated somebody had recently driven into the field. She pulled across the highway and followed the bumpy trail until they came to the cemetery.

The tall entrance arch was framed with black steel posts with white angels floating on the pillars. Overhead a steel banner proclaimed the name Four Corners Cemetery. Across the front was a recently painted rock fence which was about three feet tall. Somebody had recently mowed the grass. Remarkably everything appeared to be in good shape, considering the age of some of the head stones. At the far end there was a new grave covered with fresh flowers

Pointing to the left Sarah said, "I think Helen is over there"

"Do you want me to go see if I can find the spot and take you there?"

"Yes please if you don't mind. Everything has changed so much I'm not sure any more. I'll wait here for you in the car."

Elyse got out of the car and began walking

toward the left boundary of the cemetery. She could hear the bees buzzing in the alfalfa crop planted in the rest of the field. Not visible from the entrance, she came across a carefully cultivated flower border which defined the outer edge. After much searching, she found the barely visible stone marker with Helen's name etched on it.

Returning to the car she said to Sarah, "Hang on. I think I can drive over there and get you closer."

She drove carefully over the roots and rocks in the field in order to get as close as she possibly could to the grave site so Sarah wouldn't have to walk too far.

Helping her out of the car, she held Sarah's arm in case she tripped. While Sarah stood beside the grave Elyse wandered around the small cemetery, looking at the dates and names on the head stones. She took a picture of Sarah me kneeling by Helen's grave and another of the head stone.

As Elyse walked around the well-kept cemetery she noticed all of the graves were very old and grouped into families. There were a lot of children whose graves dated back to the same time as Helen's.

She walked over to where Gram was kneeling. "Gram," she asked, "are most of the people buried here your friends and neighbors? This is a very old cemetery and few of the graves are recent."

"Yes, I have many memories of the good people buried here. This is where I would choose to be but I already have that plot in town, can't be two places at once.

Come help me up, I am ready to go now. Getting down was easy, it's the getting up that's hard. Henry made Helen's headstone himself; we couldn't afford a store bought marker. Come over here and help me up."

Elyse patiently guided Sarah back to the car. After getting her settled she said "I am going to take a couple more pictures for you so that if you never get out here again at least you will have them." Sarah didn't seem to hear her. She was lost in her memories of how she had felt back then.

"I still miss her" she said when Elyse climbed back into the car. "When you lose a child it's as if your heart actually breaks in two, you never feel whole or complete again. You learn to live with the pain, but you never get over it. Parents should never outlive their children."

Elyse stopped and took more pictures of the entrance before turning back onto the highway. Mostly she wanted to give Gram time to compose herself.

"This is fun. Where to now Gram?" she asked lightly.

"Go back to town. I am taking you to the senior's

centre for lunch. Some of them will probably fall over when I walk in; it's been ages since I was there."

Sarah talked nonstop all the way back to town regaling her with more stories and indiscretions of her friends of long ago.

Lunch that day was one of Sarah's favourites-split pea and ham soup, and egg salad sandwiches. Elyse felt out of place because Sarah kept calling people over and introducing her.

"This is my great-granddaughter, my son Ivan's grandchild. All of this time we thought he was dead but he was alive and doing well in the states. It is a blessing she managed to find us at all."

After about an hour and a half Sarah whispered to Elyse "Do you think you could take me home now? I am feeling rather tired. This has been a big day."

Before leaving Elyse made sure Sarah was comfortable in her room. As she was walking out the door Sarah called her back. "You have made an old lady very happy today. Thank you."

She stopped at the front desk to tell the receptionist they were back. "We have had a long day and Gram is tired. Maybe you could get one of the nurses to check on her in a little while." She added.

Sarah smiled after Elyse left. *I hope that one day she understands this has been one of the best days of my life.*

Twenty Three

The insistent ringing of the motel room telephone woke Elyse from a deep sleep. Glancing at the clock radio she noticed it was eight o'clock in the morning.

"Hello," she answered sleepily. *Who could be phoning this early in the morning? Has something happened at home?*

"Elyse. This is Rachel." The quivering voice at the other end said "Mom is in the hospital."

"What happened? Is she sick? Did she fall?"

"She had stroke earlier this morning and possibly another one since arriving at the hospital. Her left side is completely paralysed. We think she can hear us but can't speak. I know she would want you to be with us at the hospital."

"I'm on my way. I should be there in about ten minutes."

Elyse quickly got out of bed, grabbed a top and pair of jeans from her suitcase and headed into the bathroom. *I'll have a quick shower and then be on my way.*

Then, like being hit by a rushing freight train, the

reality of Rachel's call hit her. She sank down to the floor of the shower, her body wracked with large gasping sobs.

No, not yet, she silently screamed. *I can't lose Gram now, I just found her. First grandfather, now Gram, where is the fairness in that?*

Still in tears she got out of the shower, dressed and ran out to her car. The traffic was light this early in the morning, and she broke the speed limit in her haste to get to the hospital. Running in the front door she said to the receptionist, "Sarah Walkers room please."

"408" replied the receptionist not looking up from her magazine. "Elevators are on the left."

Luckily there was an empty elevator waiting. Elyse pushed the button for the fourth floor then wiped her eyes with her hands. When the door opened, she took a deep breath and stepped out. The family was gathered in the hallway. Some were talking among themselves. One or two were standing away from the group, wiping tears from their eyes. Anna noticed her arrival and came to her side.

"Am I too late?" Elyse asked.

"No, but she isn't doing well. She is still with us, but seems to be drifting in and out of consciousness. It doesn't look good."

Anna led her into a private room which was softly lit by a table lamp in the corner. Elyse expected to be confronted with a vast array of machines but was surprised to see only an intravenous bottle hanging beside the bed. The only other piece of equipment was an oxygen cannula in Gram's nose.

"Mom always told us when her time came to let her go. We are merely keeping her comfortable right now."

Sarah looked so tiny laying there. Her eyes were closed, but her face looked peaceful. The red and black afghan was tucked around her and pulled up to her chin. Her breathing was so shallow Elyse had to concentrate to see the rise and fall of her chest.

"Gram," she said tentatively, "This is Elyse, I am here."

She sat down on the blue plastic chair at the side of the bed, and held the small, work-worn hand for the next several hours. A nurse came in and checked her vital signs every half hour.

Slightly after two o'clock family members began filling the room. Some sat on chairs; others on the bed, some leaned against the wall, and others stood quietly watching her sleep. Some rocked back and forth, their arms wrapped around their body as they hugged themselves. The room was silent except for the clicking of the IV monitor.

When she tried to let go of gram's hand she thought she felt the slight fingers tighten around hers. She looked at Anna helplessly. "This is not my place. One of you should be sitting here instead of me."

Rachel came over, put her arm around Elyse's shoulder and whispered into her ear. "Stay there. You made her last days very happy. You earned the right to be there."

One by one each person in the room came over, kissed Sarah on the cheek and whispered in her ear. Somehow she managed to open her eyes to look at them as they spoke to her. Some returned to their place around the bed, others slipped out into the hallway, their eyes brimming with tears.

Over the next twenty minutes her breathing slowed. Father Troy arrived and administered the last rites of the church, those still in the room prayed with him. As he finished, a tear fell from the corner of Sarah's eye, she sighed and stopped breathing.

Twenty Four

I hear the voices again. "Anna. I think has come to call the other family members. She is getting weaker by the hour."

"I have done that already. We are waiting for Father Troy to come and give her the last rites. I am sure that will comfort her, and us."

Suddenly I don't want to leave. I want to stay with my children. I want to be able to hold them in my arms one more time. Somehow, I don't know how, I managed to open my eyes. I want them to know I am still here.

I see each of them as they come to say goodbye to me. Some say I love you, others squeeze my hand and say nothing, but I can feel the love emanating from them. Others kiss my cheek, their eyes filled with tears and regret. I try to tell them not to cry, but no words come.

The last to come was Anna. "Mom we will be fine," she said." Don't try to stay for our sake. We will miss you, but we will never forget all that you have been and done for us. Without you, we wouldn't be who we are today. You are tired. Rest now, you have earned it."

I start to cry. A tear trickles from the corner of my eye and down my cheek and then I hear that booming voice, "Sarah let them go. They are all grown now. We have done all we can for them"

"Henry? Is that you?"

"We are all here mom."

At the foot of my bed stands my Henry, no longer sick and frail; Helen is there, all grown up. John too, his body no longer battered and broken.

Then I hear another voice, one I haven't heard for many years. "I'm here too mom. It has been a long time since we were together." Ivan is standing beside his father.

I smiled and reach for his hand. I hold on until Father Troy finished his prayers, and then Henry takes my hand in his and I walk away with them. I don't look back.

The last thing I hear is Elyse say, "look she is smiling".

* * *

Elyse released Sarah's hand, placed it on top of the blanket, and then slipped out of the room. *I need to be alone right now.* The family was standing around Sarah's bed; most were crying and hugging each other as they said their final good byes. Nobody noticed her leave.

She walked down to the patient lounge at the end of the hallway and stood looking out the window. Closing her eyes against the late afternoon sunshine, she visualized Gram joining Henry, John, Helen and her grandfather Ivan. In a strange way the thought of her grandfather Ivan being reunited with his mother comforted her.

When she was sure the family had left she went back into Sarah's room. She stood beside the bed and whispered "I love you Gram. Thank you for accepting me and making me a part of your family." Then she kissed her on the forehead, touched her shoulder and, with a long lingering look, walked out of the room.

Willing herself to leave the hospital she drove slowly back to the motel. Once in her room she collapsed on the bed sobbing.

Taking her cell phone out of her pants pocket Elyse called her mother. "Mom, Gram passed away a little while ago. Do you think you could come here?" They talked for several more minutes and then she disconnected her call.

Then, not knowing what else to do with herself, she got into her car and retraced the path they had travelled the day before. *Was it only yesterday we did this? We had such a good time. I never thought she would be gone today.*

Her mother arrived the day before the funeral and helped Elyse pack up her room. Later, the evening after the luncheon Rachel called. "When are you planning on going home?"

"We are leaving in the morning. Mom has to get back."

"That soon? I know it's getting late, but could you meet me in Gram's room, say in about half an hour?"

"I guess so," Elyse answered reluctantly. *I wonder what this is all about. I can't imagine going to Gram's room now that she is gone.* Once again her eyes filled with tears which she wiped away. *Crying isn't going to bring her back.*

Rachel hugged Elyse as she came through the door and introduced herself to Edna, Elyse's' mother. "You have a remarkable daughter. We are grateful for what she did for mom. I don't recall seeing her so happy since dad passed away."

They chatted for a few minutes and then Rachel walked over and took the wedding cross of the wall. "Here Elyse, this is for you. Mom told me the other day that she wanted you to have this. Mom always wanted her wedding cross passed to the oldest child's family. Ivan was her oldest child and you are his granddaughter."

"I can't take this" Elyse said handing the cross

back to Rachel. "Others deserve this more than I do."

"You can, and you will. The other family members agree with me. Mom always told us, in no uncertain terms, what she wanted done with the cross, and this is what she wanted. So please take it and treasure it." Then, she picked up the red and black afghan which had been returned to its customary place, wrapped the cross in the blanket and handed the bundle to Elyse.

"You gave her something we never could, and that was knowing where Ivan was and what happened to him. It didn't matter that he was dead; all that mattered to her was that she finally had an answer to her prayers. You will always be welcome here and will always be a member of this family."

Thank you" was all Elyse could say.

EPILOGUE

Six months later Rachel was surprised when a courier truck stopped in front of her house and unloaded a heavy box. Inside were thirty five books. The old barn from the Hines place was on the cover and the book was titled Sarah Walker, a Homesteader Story. Elyse had written Sarah's story and dedicated it to her and the family. Tears came to her eyes.

As she flipped through the pages of the book memories flooded back. *Thank you Elyse for this very special gift, we are blessed to have you as a member of our family.*

About the Author

Judy began writing as a child and then put it on hold. When she retired from sales she dusted off her dream and thought "why not?' From there nothing has held her back.

Judy lives in Alberta Canada with her husband, dog Missy Tzu, four children and four grandsons.

She can be contacted at jcoates@telusplanet.net and would appreciate hearing your comments.

.